Born in the UK, **Becky Wicks** has suffered interminable wanderlust from an early age. She's lived and worked all over the world, from London to Dubai, Sydney, Bali, NYC and Amsterdam. She's written for the likes of *GQ*, *Hello!*, *Fabulous* and *Time Out*, a host of YA romance, plus three travel memoirs—*Burqalicious*, *Balilicious* and *Latinalicious* (HarperCollins, Australia). Now she blends travel with romance for Mills & Boon and loves every minute! Tweet her @bex_wicks and subscribe at beckywicks.com.

Also by Becky Wicks

Tempted by Her Hot-Shot Doc
From Doctor to Daddy
Enticed by Her Island Billionaire

Discover more at millsandboon.co.uk.

FALLING AGAIN FOR THE ANIMAL WHISPERER

BECKY WICKS

MILLS & BOON

First published in Great Britain 2021
by Mills & Boon, an imprint of HarperCollins*Publishers* Ltd,
1 London Bridge Street, London, SE1 9GF

www.harpercollins.co.uk

HarperCollins*Publishers*
1st Floor, Watermarque Building,
Ringsend Road, Dublin 4, Ireland

Large Print edition 2021

Falling Again for the Animal Whisperer © 2021 Becky Wicks

ISBN: 978-0-263-28795-0

08/21

MIX
Paper from
responsible sources
FSC
www.fsc.org
FSC® C007454

This book is produced from independently certified
FSC™ paper to ensure responsible forest management.
For more information visit www.harpercollins.co.uk/green.

Printed and bound in Great Britain
by CPI Group (UK) Ltd, Croydon, CR0 4YY

To all the medical staff out there who have worked even more tirelessly and selflessly during the COVID-19 outbreak. Sending you thanks and love.

CHAPTER ONE

'TEMPERATURE, RESPIRATION—BOTH PERFECT. This is exactly the news we want this morning, little one.' Jodie Everleigh set their four-legged patient as straight as she could on the table in front of them. Marlow was a lot wrigglier than he had been when his owner had brought him in yesterday, which was a good sign.

The poor little Labrador puppy had been in the West Bow Vet Hospital overnight on a drip, thanks to vomiting inexplicably on his owner's kitchen floor for four days.

'He's finally eating well too,' her partner Aileen told her, easing into the exam room with two cups of coffee.

Jodie took her caffeine fix, black as usual, and watched as Aileen ruffled the pup's soft golden fur around his ears, prompting him to try and lick her face from the table.

'Did I tell you how grateful I am that you're

as good at knowing when I need coffee as you are with the animals?' she told her, noting the rain start up again over Edinburgh's glum-looking streets out the window. Aileen gave her the thumbs up over the puppy and Jodie smiled, stifling a yawn. They'd built this practice together from the ground up, and their staff had become her second family.

'If he keeps his breakfast down without any vomiting, we might get to send him home this afternoon,' she said, checking the schedule quickly on the iPad on the wall. 'I'll check on our kitten Simba back there. Mark will be in at noon, so he'll do the dog booster vaccinations and...'

'Anika can do the rabbit nail clip if you have to pick Emmie up from the stables,' Aileen finished.

'She might have to,' Jodie replied, thinking back in slight dismay to this morning's argument with her daughter Emmie. She'd promised to go riding with her but she'd been so busy she'd forgotten, and Emmie had run to her father, citing her a bad mother. She knew Emmie didn't mean it. She was just an impassioned preteen whose body was changing as fast as her opinion on who was the better parent.

Ethan probably had been, lately, she mused. Her ex-husband had a new girlfriend, Saskia, who seemed to have boundless energy as well as a love of horses. While Jodie was happy for her ex-husband, it didn't escape her how she herself seemed to live for work and not much else lately—but what was she supposed to do? She was a single mother, and she'd worked damn hard to provide Emmie and herself with the life they both loved here.

Jodie's phone buzzed. Her father. 'Hey, Dad, sorry I've not called this week. I've been swamped—'

'Jodie, I'm afraid it's not good news. Are you sitting down?'

'Oh, God, what?' She dropped heavily to the swivel chair behind the desk and braced herself. 'It's not Mum, is it?'

Her dad sounded frazzled, tired. 'Mum's fine. It's my brother…your uncle Casper.'

'Casper?'

'He died last night, Jodie. He had a heart attack on the estate at Everleigh…' Her father trailed off, seemingly trying to compose himself. Her heart was thudding suddenly, like that of a rabbit kicking its way through her ribcage. Uncle Casper was *dead*?

Her palm turned sweaty around the phone. She hadn't seen Casper in years, not since her wedding, but he'd been a staple in her life all through her childhood. She'd pretty much grown up on his estate around his veterinary practice and horses in Dorset. 'Dad, I'm so sorry,' she managed.

'The funeral is on Friday. Cole called me with the news.'

Her head was spinning harder now, making it hard to breathe. 'Cole Crawford called you?'

She felt glued to her swivel seat. 'He didn't call me,' she found herself saying, and then wondered why she was surprised. Why the hell would Cole Crawford call her? He hadn't called her in twelve years, not since he'd announced, right before they'd been due to leave for Edinburgh, *together*, that he wouldn't be joining her there.

Her father relayed the funeral details and she only half heard them.

Already the memories were flooding her brain

like tidal waves—her funny, witty, wealthy, horse-mad uncle Casper was dead, and Cole, her first love, her first everything, had called her father with the news, which meant he was probably still working at Casper's estate.

She hung up, thoughts reeling.

She could still see Cole's face as clear as day. The way it had changed from that of an eleven-year-old boy to a nineteen-year-old man over endless long summers in Dorset. She'd lived for them, the same way he'd seemed to live only for Casper's horses when they'd first met. His compassion for the animals had rubbed off on her and led her to where she was today.

She could see the look in Cole's brown, soulful eyes at fifteen years old, kissing her for the first time. Sixteen years old, telling her he loved her. And then…nineteen years old, telling her he wouldn't be going to Edinburgh with her, to vet school, like they'd planned. Before that moment, when he'd destroyed *all* their future plans together, she'd assumed she'd met the love of her life.

She'd begged to know what had happened, why he was changing his mind about vet school, and Edinburgh, and her. She'd never got any answers.

The last thing she wanted to do, she realised, was see Cole Crawford again.

CHAPTER TWO

THE RAIN WAS sheeting down in hard diagonal slashes as Cole steered the Land Rover down the single-track country road. The puddles reared up around the wheels, sending vertical mudslides up the sides, right up to the windows. February in Dorset was always like this but the daffodils were poking their heads up already.

'Spring's here, somewhere,' he muttered to Ziggy, eyes on the road. 'We have to see how this one goes without Casper, huh?'

His faithful Border collie and respected veterinary assistant lolled his tongue out on the passenger seat beside him. Ziggy had been travelling these roads, doing the house calls with him, ever since he was a pup. Cole was grateful for his company today.

He'd kept himself to himself and the animals more than usual, he supposed, since Casper's death. He still didn't know if he'd processed it. Casper's heart had simply given up, right there on the spot. He'd been seventy-two years old and fighting fit, or so everyone had thought.

'You never know when it's coming,' he said out loud over the steering wheel. Ziggy looked at him blankly. And then, out of nowhere, Jodie was back in his mind.

He'd been getting these 'hits' of her since he'd called her father with the news. He knew they'd both be at the funeral and the thought of seeing her face up close, twelve years after he'd broken things off with her, wasn't sitting too well at all. Not that she didn't have a beautiful face…but the last time he'd seen it she'd been crushed and furious. She'd looked at him like he was ripping her heart out from her chest with a meat hook and later the absence of her had left him feeling just as hollow.

Jodie.

He'd be saying her name again a lot in a matter of days, talking to her face to face, looking straight into those eyes. All the shades of blue, warm like the ocean in summer. They'd been like anchors to him once. They'd probably be as cold as ice now, he thought wryly, considering how he'd left things. They'd been through so much. He'd been through more than she knew without her…although he was sure getting married and having a kid had kept her more than busy.

Life had been tough for him before Jodie had entered his life in a riot of city girl attitude, aged eleven, the same as him. His parents' berry farm, Thistles, was struggling back then and he'd known things were very wrong even before his father had been locked away for tax evasion. Most fathers didn't welcome their sons home at the end of the day with a bottle of whisky and two fists to use on a kid's face. He'd never told anyone. The guy had been a waste of space right up to the day he'd died, six months after he'd got out of jail. Jodie had been gone by then, pregnant, on the verge of getting married.

Ziggy barked as he swerved to avoid a pothole and he hit the gas harder. 'I've got it, buddy.'

The cow was waiting in agony at Rob Briar's dairy farm; this rain wouldn't stop him hurrying, but images of Jodie were coming thick and fast, threatening to break his focus. The photo of her in the wedding dress had killed him— some posh politician's son had swept her off her high-heeled feet. It was his own fault he'd lost her, but pregnant and married after six months of college? Crazy.

He could still hear Casper telling him the news. *Jodie's pregnant. She met a Scotsman up there, it seems pretty serious. She's going to marry him.'*

She'd always been his. Even when he'd broken things off for her own safety, he'd stupidly assumed she'd be his again when he'd figured out how to handle things at home, or at least created a safe environment to bring her back to. He'd used to love the way Jodie Everleigh took him by surprise, but a wedding and a baby at nineteen…he'd never expected *that*.

Twelve years earlier

'So, are you excited, Cole? It's going to be an adventure. Did you see the rooms are all ready for us in Waverleigh House? It's the best student house in Edinburgh.'

Jodie went on and on, babbling excitedly the way she did, and Cole felt the ball of angst fill his stomach like a lead balloon.

She was about to leave Everleigh again. They were sitting on the hay bales outside the stables, waiting for her car. In minutes it would pull up on the gravel and take her to the train station, and he still hadn't been able to tell her what had happened.

He'd been putting his news off all weekend. How could he crush her by telling her he couldn't come to Edinburgh, or university, because of his father? She didn't even know how violent the man really was; he'd been locked up for the last four and a half years, the whole time they'd been an item.

She knew he was serving time for tax evasion, but no one knew about the physical abuse he and his mother had endured before that.

Jodie was still talking, one leg draped over his lap in her jeans, resting against his shoulder. Their fingers were laced together. He'd never said it, he wasn't so great with words, but he didn't think he'd ever fit with anyone the way he fitted with Jodie.

Suddenly, she was frowning at him, trying to read him. 'What's wrong? You've been weird all weekend.'

'Jodie.' He swallowed, extracting himself from her and pulling his knees up to his chest. Her bags were at their feet. Everleigh's driveway was still empty but the sky was darkening above them, almost like the heavens were preparing for his fate. He drew a long breath, rammed his hands in his hair. 'I'm not coming with you to Edinburgh. I'm sorry.'

Jodie laughed. 'Very funny. As if you could live without me...' She leaned in to kiss him again but he turned his face away.

He said nothing, racking his brain as to how to explain it without sounding weak and pathetic. He knew he should have stood up to his father's violence years ago, but when they'd locked him up, he'd been so relieved to finally be free of him that he'd lost himself in Jodie, finally.

He hadn't thought about when he'd be released, or that he might get out early and come home even angrier than before. He hadn't predicted his own mother would welcome him back so eagerly either, but she'd always been even weaker around the man than *him*.

'Cole?' The colour had drained from Jodie's face. She blinked at him. 'You're serious. You're not coming?'

'I can't, Jodie.'

She pursed her lips, stepped back and crossed her arms, then uncrossed them quickly, flustered. 'Why? Cole, you already have a place. I thought we were doing this together. I know it's all a big change but, come on, it's the Royal School of Veterinary Studies, it's the best. And we can come back down here whenever we want for the weekends and holidays...'

When his father would be waiting to mess them both up. 'No. Listen to me, Jodie, it's not the right time.'

Cole had already been accused of turning his father back to drink. Funny, that. There had been no alcohol in the house when he'd come home from prison via the pub, steaming drunk.

Now there were beer cans all over the living room and Cole had spent the whole weekend hiding the bruise on his right thigh from Jodie. It had throbbed for hours after the TV had crashed into him, then shattered on the floor tiles. Luckily his mother had been out. All Cole had done was explain that his place in Edinburgh was set in stone, and he was leaving with Jodie at the end of the month.

His father had been quick to stomp on his plans as much as the broken television: *'I need you here around the farm. How dare you think you can just leave without earning your keep?'*

He'd already pulled the funding reserved for his studies. His callous actions made Cole's teeth start to grind all over again.

'What's going on?' Jodie's blue eyes were imploring. He should just tell her.

But he'd already been over this with himself. If he told Jodie, she would storm over to his house and confront his father, and he couldn't put her in the line of fire like that. She might also ask her rich dad or Casper to help, which of course they would, and his father would go crazy if anyone tried to pull him away from here now.

Jodie had no clue the abuse people suffered whenever his dad got angry. He'd never told *anyone*.

'Tell anyone and I'll kill you,' his dad would rage, seconds after landing a punch on him, or throwing him against a wall, or sending a bottle flying at his head from across the kitchen. The TV was nothing, he'd done worse than that before over the years. What if he struck out at Jodie now he was home? The thought made him go cold.

'Maybe I'll defer a year, I don't know,' he said now. In the distance a horse let out a whinny.

'I'll defer a year too, then,' she shot back.

Dammit. He should have known she would say that. 'No, Jodie.'

She looked at him in defiance. 'Well, I'm not going without you.'

'You have to go, Jodie, it's all you've talked about for years.'

'It's all *we've* talked about for years. We were going to study together, and then come back here, work on the rescue centre, more horses like Mustang. What's happened?' She reached for his face. Tears were pooling in her eyes now and it almost broke him. 'Cole, what's happened?'

'Nothing,' he lied.

'I love you,' she said. Her eyes said she expected to hear the truth.

He just shook his head.

'Talk to me.' Jodie gripped his hair either side of his head, drew him closer. He could feel her hands shaking. 'Talk to me. I just told you I love you. Why won't you say it back?'

Because if I do, I won't be able to let you go. The voice in his head was raging. He loved her so much it hurt but he had to put her safety first, and her education. She wanted to go to vet school so badly, she was so excited. He wouldn't let her risk all that just to be with him in the mess he'd created. He had to stay here for a while at least, keep his mother safe, figure out his next steps.

'You don't love me? You don't want to be with me? Is *that* why you're pulling out of coming to Edinburgh?' Confusion flooded Jodie's eyes. Cole fought not to press his thumbs to the tears streaming down her cheeks but he dug his nails into his palms and forced himself not to move. He'd crack the moment he touched her. Jodie deserved better than this.

'I'm sorry,' he said, forcing his eyes to the floor. 'We're going in different directions.'

'What? I don't understand what's happening, Cole!'

The car's headlights behind her turned her trembling body into a silhouette and he felt the loss of her overwhelm him instantly. He almost reached for her again. He almost told her that of course he loved her, that he was trying to *protect* her. But maybe it was better this way. She wouldn't stay for anyone who didn't want her. She'd be safer and the further away she was from here and him the better.

The silence was excruciating. The car pulled up and the driver rolled the window down. 'Train station, love?'

Jodie lowered her voice, eyes glistening. 'You waited all weekend to break up with me right at the last minute?' She sounded angry now, fuming, humiliated. He focused on his breathing, tried to stay cool. 'I can't believe this,' she hissed.

'I'm sorry.'

Jodie started scrambling for her bags. He jumped down and went to help her but she shoved at his chest, forcing him back onto the hay bale with a strength that surprised him. 'No!'

She flung the car door open and launched herself into the back seat, slamming it after her. 'You know where I'll be when you come to your senses,' she said through the window. 'And if you don't, it's your loss, Cole Crawford.'

CHAPTER THREE

'THIS WEATHER! Is it always like this here?'
Emmie looked affronted in the passenger seat
and Jodie almost let out a laugh.

They were somewhere on a rural road between Weymouth and Dorchester, but things
looked different from how she remembered.
There were more sheds, more farms, more cot-
tages between the villages, out in the sticks.
There was definitely more rain.

'It's not like this in the summertime,' she told
her daughter, which was true. 'You should see
the flowers here usually, all around the ditches.
There's yellow flag, great willowherb, meadow-
sweet, purple loosestrife…' She listed a bunch
that Cole had told her the names of once.

Emmie wrinkled her nose at the snowflakes
that were now flurrying down on the windows
instead of rain. She clearly didn't care about the
flowers, and was already missing her horse,
Saxon.

Up ahead, the traffic had almost ground to a halt. Jodie glanced at the clock on the dashboard. The funeral was in two hours. They were just a few miles from the estate but if it didn't clear up, they might be late.

'We're going to be late,' Emmie announced unnecessarily, pulling out her phone for the hundredth time. Seconds later she moaned, 'Mum, there's no signal here.'

'It'll come back,' Jodie told her, hoping it was true. She had to call into West Bow soon and make sure things were OK. She was full of butterflies. Scowling at the snow, she knew she could tell herself the butterflies were because of so many things, but who was she kidding? She was about to see Cole again. The thought had left her tossing and turning all night in the hotel bed.

A tractor crawled up alongside them, urging her further towards the roadside. The snow was coming down heavier now. It was almost a blizzard. With despair she noticed the signal must have died on her phone too and messed up the GPS. The map had sent them down a wrong one-way road.

'Dammit,' she cursed in frustration, swiping

her scarf over her shoulder with her loose hair. She needed to go back, but there was nowhere to turn.

Emmie rolled her eyes. 'Way to go, Mum.'

Jodie's stomach was in knots. She didn't even have the energy to tell Emmie not to be so rude. She already knew her daughter didn't want to be here, but with Ethan and his girlfriend going away for a long weekend she'd had no choice but to take Emmie out of school and bring her.

'This is the worst day ever,' Emmie grumbled, tapping in vain at her phone screen. 'We could have spent this weekend riding Saxon! I didn't even know your uncle Casper.'

'Actually, you did meet Casper once,' Jodie said, distracted. 'You were just very small, that's all. In fact, you hadn't even been born.'

'Gross!'

Emmie had been a tiny bulge in her wedding gown the last time she'd seen Casper. He had tried to seem happy for her the whole time, but she'd known deep down he hadn't been. She'd caught her uncle looking between her and Ethan, like he was trying and failing to spot the same kind of connection he'd often commented on between herself and Cole. He'd always thought of Cole like the son he'd never had. He'd also watched them fall madly in love. She guessed her uncle had always assumed it would be her and Cole having a baby together, eventually. Not that she could ever regret having had Emmie.

Averting her eyes back to the road, she recalled the moment she'd pulled up the pregnancy test to find the tiny blue line. It had been a signal that her life was about to change once again.

She'd still been heartbroken over Cole ending their relationship when the accident had happened. Had it been vodka or tequila she and Ethan had been glugging like water when they'd ended up in bed, blurring the lines of their friendship and setting the life-changing chain of events in motion? She couldn't even remember now.

Ethan's father had been on the verge of being re-elected for the fourth time—everyone had known who the Labour MP was, and everyone had known his son, too. The election had already been a roller-coaster for the whole family. Ethan had been under huge pressure to stay out of the limelight, not to screw up his studies, or his life. It was the reason he'd been drowning his own sorrows alongside her behind the closed doors of their shared student flat that night.

Jodie hadn't ever come under quite that much pressure. If anything, perfection to her busy screenwriting, jet-setting parents was having her out of their hair for seven years while she completed her degree. But she'd *wanted* to complete her studies to the best of her ability; vet school had been her dream for as long as she could remember.

When she'd discovered she was pregnant—from the one night in her life she hadn't used contraception—neither she nor Ethan had wanted to abandon their studies. But they'd refused to abort the baby.

'You'll live to regret it, if you have this baby,' her mother had said.

But she'd stood her ground. She'd known she'd live to regret it if she *didn't*.

Ethan had been supportive, but they'd both known they couldn't study *and* raise a child with no help.

It had come as a surprise when their parents had joined forces and offered to finance a home and childcare so they could finish their degrees and keep the baby...with one small caveat from Ethan's father. They had to marry. A twenty-year-old son with a baby out of wedlock would not have looked good on an MP's campaign trail.

Looking back, she knew she should never have agreed to such a ludicrous suggestion. She was still ashamed of how she'd bowed in submission, but she'd cared for Ethan more than for herself at the time, she supposed. She had been lost, naive and still grieving for Cole. Ethan had been her good friend; appeasing their families had also been making the best of a bad situation. They'd been sure they could make it work and divorce quietly a few years later. What was a marriage certificate anyway? Just a piece of paper.

To this day, only their families and closest friends knew the deal they'd struck. For a second she wondered if Cole had ever questioned her marrying Ethan so young; or wished things had worked out between *them*.

Don't be ridiculous, she scolded herself. *He didn't try to contact you once after breaking up with you! He never even tried to come to Ed-*

inburgh in the end. Why would he care if you got married...or divorced?

Jodie reached for her coffee cup, before remembering it had been empty for almost three hours. She was so far from home already—there was no going back.

It's only two nights, she told herself, trying to stay calm as she slowed the car a metre behind the tractor. She'd booked them into The Ship Inn—a fifteenth-century hotel a mile from Everleigh Estate. Even the thought of staying in the same area as Cole Crawford for the weekend was making her feel queasy.

'So, was Casper married?' Emmie asked now.

'Nope,' she said, squinting through the snow. 'Some people said he was married to his horses.'

'Who will be looking after them now he's gone?'

'I assume he has staff,' she answered, though she had been wondering herself how the inheritance would be split and what would become of Everleigh. No one had mentioned his will yet, which surprised her. Her father would have said something surely, if he knew.

The snow was coming down even thicker now, huge white blobs battling with the windshield wipers. The sat-nav still wasn't working properly and she was about ready to crack when eventually, after crawling the Peugeot along like a caterpillar, she found a place ahead to turn around.

They'd only just made it past a rickety cattle grid when the car engine spluttered to a stop.

The snow shouldn't make him too late, Cole thought. The Land Rover had got them through worse than this. He only worried for the people on their way to the funeral. Over five hundred attendees were supposed to be showing up at two p.m. *Including Jodie.*

Ziggy started barking manically over the radio. Frowning, he slowed the vehicle, feeling the tyres crunch on the fresh snow. Ziggy never barked unless he was alerting him to danger.

Then he saw the silver car through the blizzard. It was almost invisible, the windshield covering fast with snow. Clearly the wipers weren't working.

'They must have broken down,' he said to Ziggy.

He steered the Land Rover past the car and noted two figures in the front. He wasn't sure, but he thought he could make out a woman and a young girl. Jumping out into the blizzard, his boots made fresh dents in the tyre marks as he strode to the back and pulled his tow rope from the boot.

A woman was standing in the snow now.

'The engine just died,' she called out, squinting through the flurry. He pulled his hat down against the snow and held up the tow rope.

He couldn't see her face but she was standing half-sheltered by the open car door. He fought a smile at her tight denim jeans tucked into unscuffed, too-clean brown leather boots. She clearly wasn't from around here.

Cole was at the car door in seconds, peering around her at the kid first, checking she was OK. Her long blonde hair looked freshly brushed and she commanded his gaze with big restless ocean-blue eyes. She was what…ten? Eleven?

'Can you help us, please? We're late to a funeral,' the woman said from the confines of a giant red woollen scarf. He pushed his hat up and stepped back to look at her. Her eyes grew round, just as his throat grew tight. 'Cole?'

Jodie.

Her face was as white as the snow, or maybe more ashen. Damn, he thought, taking her all in up close with the snow settling on her hair. Here she was, right in front of him, out of the blue. The kid…was her daughter, he realised now.

He was half smiling again, more out of shock than anything, but he only realised this when he met Jodie's narrowed eyes. Ice-blue, just like the last time she'd looked at him, pleading for answers. He tried not to let on the whirlwind in his brain that had replaced all regular cognitive behaviour. 'Cole…can you just help us?'

Her voice was trembling slightly as she shut the door. She almost caught her sweater sleeve in it and he heard her tut in annoyance. She was nervous, agitated, like a cornered deer with nowhere to run.

Age hadn't changed her much, he noted. He'd feigned indifference back then but the first time he'd laid eyes on her she'd been the most exotic thing he'd ever seen, and she'd seemed disarmingly unaware of how pretty she was. It was like Casper had invited a rare creature onto the estate that, for once, he'd had no clue what to do with.

The young kid wound the window down, and stuck her head out. 'You know this man, Mum?'

'One second, sweetheart.'

He heard Jodie suck in a breath as she followed him to the back of the car. She was hugging her arms around herself against the cold or the shock of seeing him sooner than expected, maybe both.

She opened her mouth to speak but a motorcyclist slipped past their vehicles and sped off too fast. The action sent a cold slushy shower of muddy water over them and Jodie shrieked.

He dropped the tow rope and reached for her at the same time as she stumbled against him. In a second he was holding her too tightly at the side of the road. Some protective impulse had kicked in, like the time he'd yanked her from Mustang's path. The new rescue horse could have mown her down if he hadn't seen it coming and jumped the fence.

'Cole,' she whispered shakily against him. Her palms were pressed flat against his chest over his jacket. She drew long, slow, deep breaths under his chin like she was struggling for air. A long-extinguished fire began to smoke from the depths of his core as his fingers scrunched into a tumble of soft, damp hair that made the past fly back in a heartbeat.

It was maybe three…four long seconds before she pulled back from him, swiping in vain at her muddy jeans, avoiding his eyes. She was soaked and so was he, not that he'd noticed till now. Time was unwinding. Her honey-brown waves were springing into curls, like her hair always had when it had got wet.

He found his voice, adjusted his hat. 'You'll dry off.'

'It's not like I'm not always covered in mud, whenever I'm around you,' she replied. Then she scowled to herself, like she'd sworn she wouldn't remind herself, or him, of anything to do with their past. He was sure they *both* knew that wasn't going to be easy, but then she *was* only staying a couple of days at most so how hard would it be just to stay out of each other's way?

Right after he got her out of this mess.

The towing interface came out easily from its compartment in the back. He could almost feel Jodie's eyes appraising his muddy boots and jacket from behind him as he screwed it in place. He caught her daughter's gaze in the wing mirror.

So this was Ethan Sanders's daughter. Ethan was an equine dental vet. Cole had looked him up years ago in a moment of curiosity, right after he'd come home from his last stint in Sri Lanka and broken things off with Diyana. Jodie didn't know about Diyana. He assumed not anyway, unless Casper had mentioned it.

As much as it had pained him over the years, he was glad Jodie had married someone who'd gone on to be successful. It wasn't his business, but he wondered why their marriage had ended.

His heart was like a wild horse throwing a fit in his chest now. That...*thing*...whatever it was between him and Jodie that he'd felt the first time he'd kissed her had thrown him off guard. He'd felt something reconnecting the second he'd pulled her head under his chin again; two live wires fusing back together.

He caught himself. It was all in his head. She was getting to him already. 'We should go, Jodie. We both have somewhere to be. Attach this to the back of your car.'

She took the rope he held out to her and he watched her drag a hand nervously through her long hair. 'The funeral, will we make it on time? Emmie and I still have to get to The Ship Inn, we need to change…'

'Forget that.' He made for the Land Rover with the other end of the tow rope, wiping his snowy hands on his jeans. 'No time. You'll just have to come with me.'

CHAPTER FOUR

THE REST OF the day was a blur to Jodie. Five hundred expected guests had become three hundred after the church ceremony and burial because of the weather. There were still more people than she'd ever seen in the huge farm-house.

The kitchen was as she remembered it, as warm and inviting as ever, with its dark wooden beams laden with pots and pans and the fire blazing in the hearth. Cole, however, sent a chill right through her.

He'd changed into a navy-blue suit and tie. She couldn't help noticing the aristocratic cut of an expert tailor, which surprised her somewhat as it spoke of a man with money. Lots of it. To anyone else the suit would highlight his chis-elled features, piercing brown eyes and shrewd mind, but to her, the whole look hid the real him. Cole might have money now but he was anything but a suit and business guy.

Jodie looked away. She didn't know him any more, and she didn't particularly want to, but she'd bet her last banknote his life was a revolving door of mud and mayhem and horses and avoiding small talk...or any kind of talk, she thought in a flicker of fresh irritation at how he'd ended things with her.

'It's good to see you, Crawford.' Her father, with his freshly shaven jaw set in stern contemplation, was resting one hand on the end of the marble centre island. From his seat on one of the bar stools, Cole nodded bluntly at the obvious lie. Her father had never approved of him—he'd once remarked that Cole had his head in the clouds and would never be able to support her.

'I know you were close to my brother, Crawford,' her father continued. 'I hear he pulled some strings to get you a scholarship in London after you ducked out of going to Edinburgh with Jodie?'

Jodie felt her cheeks blaze at the dig on her behalf, and she hid behind a bite of her puff pastry canapé. If this was her father's way of reprimanding Cole for treating her poorly he didn't have to, especially not today of all days. Although she couldn't deny that she *was* interested to hear what he'd say.

'That's correct.' Cole seemed unfazed by the dig. Maybe he hadn't even noticed it. He reached a hand down to pet Ziggy. 'I owe a lot to Casper. I worked hard for him but you're right, his contacts in London helped with my scholarship. I also trained here at Everleigh in the summers, when I wasn't in Sri Lanka. And I came right back after I graduated. That was always the plan.'

Her father was nodding politely but Jodie felt the bad blood simmer in her veins again. How dared he talk about his 'plan' with Casper when he'd pulled the plans they'd made together right out from under her? Also...*he'd been in Sri Lanka?* What on earth had taken him there?

'This was always more of a home to me than Thistles. Casper was kind of a father figure to me, I'm sure you know that.' Cole reached for the bowl of peanuts on the counter. He scooped a handful into his mouth and she heard them crunch, feeling his eyes on her. Was he thinking she looked different now? Better or worse?

Why should she care?

'I was sorry to hear about Jack,' her dad continued, and Cole frowned, filling the space with even more awkwardness. She knew Cole's father had never even met her dad. The only time she'd seen Jack herself had been when the cops had dragged him off in handcuffs. They'd been fourteen, summer had just begun, and she'd followed the sound of the sirens across the adjoining fields to Thistles.

Cole had held her back at the gate. Jack had been blind drunk, struggling with the authorities. He'd ended up serving time for tax evasion, something about stashing funds in a foreign account. She'd never got the details. Cole wouldn't talk about it, not that he'd ever talked about his dad a lot *before* he'd been arrested either. Or any of his family. He really had just seemed to live for his horses.

'How did he die?' she asked now, feeling slightly guilty that she hadn't called him when she'd heard about Jack passing away.

Cole met her eyes. 'He was taking a leak into the River Stour. Guess he didn't realise where the edge was.'

'He *drowned*?' Jodie felt terrible. Cole just nodded, his face not giving anything away.

'And your mother?' she pressed, cursing the fact that her mouth was asking questions when she'd told her mind not to care about his life at all. His mother had always been sweet to her. She had been a quiet, meek little thing, wouldn't say boo to a goose. 'How is she?'

'Loving life, thank you,' Cole said. His face softened slightly 'After my dad was found dead she lived here at Everleigh for a few months. Then she met a guy called Darren at the organic market. They run a mixed farm of arable, sheep and beef now down in Puddletown.'

'That sounds nice for her and… Darren, was it?' her father said, feigning interest. Jodie had almost forgotten he was there, but she felt her mouth twitch in spite of her mood. Her dad wouldn't know a dairy heifer from a chocolate milkshake and he had little interest in farmers, or anything they stood for. Casper had had chickens, pigs and horses, a sprawling estate and a successful veterinary practice in the countryside. Michael Everleigh had accolades and trophies and first-class tickets to movie premieres.

Her mother, Vivian, was the other half of their successful screenwriting duo and the three of them had lived in Greenwich since she was born. The Everleigh brothers couldn't have been more different if they'd tried. Looking at her father now, Jodie realised he hadn't *disliked* Cole. He'd just never really understood him. Not like *she* did…or thought she had, once.

From the second she'd met Cole she'd been fascinated, even though he'd shown no real interest in her that first summer. His indifference had only fascinated her more because he hadn't been like the boys at her school. She could still recall the moment she'd first laid eyes on his wild black, untamed curls and muddy jeans.

Cole had rescued wild horses with Casper and ridden them bareback, barefoot. He'd had zero interest in TV or any other gadgets but he'd known how to drive a tractor and milk a goat. He'd liked reading big, wordy books by writers like Tolstoy, Hemingway and Shakespeare, which she'd thought odd because he'd never had too many words to share himself. And he'd spent most of his nights in the stables, turning pages, tuning in to the horses.

His quietness had made him observant of everything, especially around the animals. She'd seen the proof many times that he'd had a real gift for picking up on the tiniest shifts in their behaviour and demeanour. He'd made countless diagnoses out on calls and around the estate way before Casper had even made any examinations.

To Jodie he'd been a mystery. A welcome distraction from the fact that she'd been deposited with her uncle Casper purely so her parents could get rid of her for the summer. He was a still a mystery now, she mused, noting how his new short beard lined his lips—lips she'd once kissed hungrily, lazily, desperately, in every way possible, for hours on end.

Cole's phone buzzed. 'It's the solicitor,' he told them after a moment. 'I bet she can't make it through this snow to read the will.'

'Shame, that, seeing as *no* one knows what my brother put in that will yet,' her dad grumbled. 'I'm probably the allocated executor,' he continued, 'and I really have to leave right after this.'

Jodie met Cole's eyes, wincing at her father's words. He clearly expected to have inherited the estate, being Casper's only sibling. Yet he was still putting his work schedule first.

'Excuse me a moment,' Cole said. He slid

off his school and moved to the corner of the kitchen by the copper sink. Jodie watched Ziggy pad after him, wishing she wasn't still so sucked in by his infuriating handsomeness. Cole's commanding bone structure and the nose that ended bluntly instead of in a point gave him as much character as his new beard. His whole persona spoke of a life outdoors in the elements, and she shivered in the warm kitchen, recalling the feeling back at the car of being in his arms again.

She'd wanted to feel repulsed, but she'd stuck to him like a magnet for far longer than necessary. It had felt like that, at least.

His conversation seemed to last a while. She kept one eye on Emmie, who was chatting to a young boy about her age over by the roaring fireplace. But whenever she glanced at him, Cole seemed to be watching her, nodding, as if his conversation involved her somehow. Or maybe he was simply appraising this new, older version of someone he'd once known so well, the same as she was doing with him.

Had he ever thought about her when he'd been studying in London, instead of Edinburgh? Or in Sri Lanka? She'd never been anywhere that exotic.

Where else in the world had he been while she and Ethan had been rained into an Edinburgh townhouse, surrounded by nappies and baby toys? They'd had childcare and assistance, thanks to their parents, but their lives hadn't exactly been like most students' lives for the seven years they'd worked on their degrees.

Not that Cole was entirely to blame for her pregnancy…it could just as easily have been *his* child she'd conceived, she supposed. Even though they'd always been careful. She'd only been off the Pill a couple of months when she'd slept with Ethan and they'd both been so incredibly drunk it was a miracle they'd even figured out what went where.

Cole caught her eyes again. Annoyed, she averted her gaze and reached for another canapé. All the times they'd had sex on this property, they'd 'christened' pretty much every room. It had been by far the best sex of her life. She suddenly felt hot in her tight black dress. She didn't want to find anything attractive about Cole but it was like asking a toddler not to like ice cream.

Jodie watched Cole pull on his plaid jacket and a thick woollen scarf.

Finally off the phone, she expected him to try and sneak off unseen, just him and his dog. Instead, he signalled for her to follow him outside into the snow.

The log cabin on the path towards the stables must have been at least fifteen feet long. It was sheltered by swaying oaks and sycamores, a peaceful oasis made entirely of thick knotted tree trunks and weathered oak panels. Jodie pulled her jacket tighter around her black lace dress as Cole led them to a stop outside the window.

'This wasn't here before,' she observed, as the snow swirled around them and settled on the cherry trees in the garden. 'Wasn't this just a field?'

'Yes,' he said. 'I built it here because of the trees. Gives me more privacy.'

'You built it yourself?'

He laughed softly. 'I had some help. We took reclaimed steel sash windows from at least five different projects in the area. Would've gone to waste otherwise.'

'Good to hear you're such an eco-warrior,' she quipped, aware that her nerves around him were making her prickly. He'd done a good job. The place had clearly cost a lot of money, humble as it appeared.

'I work out the back; we had another consultation space built with access right onto the paddocks.'

'What do you do here exactly?'

'Behavioural therapy, with horses mostly. People come to me with all kinds of animals. They just started showing up at the main house and it got a little much. So we began redirecting them here.'

'Behavioural therapy, huh?' Jodie was letting it all sink in. It shouldn't surprise her that people sought Cole out. He was better at reading animals than any vet she'd ever met.

A light inside the cabin illuminated a fireplace as they passed a window. She made out a comfy-looking long couch and a sheepskin rug. The shelves around the fireplace were piled with books. Tolstoy, Hemingway, Shakespeare… All the classics he'd always been buried in, still within reach. No TV.

She wouldn't say it out loud, but they both

knew Cole had built this cabin just where they'd imagined 'their retreat' would be. Her stomach churned as he led her onwards, but she couldn't help stopping by the snow-covered stone benches laid out in a semi-circle around one side of the firepit. They'd put cushions over those in the summer, years ago.

'Casper always loved that fire pit,' she said.

Cole stopped beside her in the snow, sighing in nostalgia. 'He did.'

They were both silent for a moment, remembering her uncle. He'd been the king of toasting marshmallows. 'It's so strange, being here without him,' she said quietly, swallowing a lump in her throat.

'Tell me about it.' Cole eyed her sideways. She noticed his fingers twitching at his sides before he shoved them in his pockets. 'We need to talk, Jodie.'

Discomfort crossed his handsome features, making her heart start to thrum. She swallowed again, a mix of tears and nerves. Of course they needed to talk. They both knew they had unresolved issues.

'What about?' she said anyway. She'd let him start with an apology. He owed her that much for the stone-cold silence that had tormented her like a ghost, after he'd watched her drive off in that taxi. She'd told him to come and find her when he came to his senses, but he never had.

He was looking at her now the way he'd looked at her before, she realised, when he'd delivered the most terrible news. She felt a little queasy. 'Let's go somewhere warmer,' he suggested.

At the heavy wooden doors to the stables Cole ushered her inside away from the elements and pressed a booted foot to the door behind them, closing it with a bang. The wind reached through the gap beneath like icy fingers, blowing at a half-empty hay net on the wall.

Jodie's teeth began to chatter as the sweet, damp smell of grass and ammonia rattled her memory bank. They'd sheltered from a summer storm in here once, and had made love against the creaking fences of empty stalls, and behind hay bales, even on the seat of the old rusting tractor. The rain on the corrugated iron roof had been like a barrage of deafening bullets, concealing their moans of pleasure.

'So...you wanted to talk,' she said, wishing the memories weren't so vivid in his presence.

Cole's deep brown eyes narrowed, forcing his brows to meet beneath his hat. Saying nothing, he uncoiled his scarf. Before she could refuse he looped the thick, black woollen warmth of it around her neck and she prayed he wouldn't hear her heart thudding wildly in the silence.

'Come,' he said. 'There's someone who wants to see you.'

He led her along the gated stalls. There was a horse in each one, but he stopped at the second to last in line. Jodie almost teared up again at the sight of their horse. 'Mustang is still here?'

'Where else would he be?'

Cole lifted the bar at the stall door. The top half was pinned back by an iron hook and the huge black stallion stopped his graceful grazing on a pile of sweet grass to look at her. He was older and slower now, Jodie noticed with a pang... The horse, not Cole.

Cole was bigger and stronger and broader and he filled her with as much apprehension as ever. She watched him in the lowlight, holding out his palm, letting Mustang snuffle him.

Damn him for looking so good next to a horse. The only thing hotter was watching him tame one. He looked good with a beard, she mused again before she could remind herself not to think such things. She knew the coarse hairs along his jaw hid a small scar on his chin. He'd said he'd got it slipping on seaweed, foraging for winkles one summer when he was ten.

'He remembers you,' Cole told her, without looking away from Mustang.

'I'm sure he does.' Jodie followed him into the stall. She'd always been in awe of their relationship—Cole had brought Mustang to the estate from a government enclosure, after he'd been herded with a pack of wild horses to make way for agricultural land. Mustang had been bucking wild when he'd arrived. Cole had been the only one able to get close.

Mustang took a step towards her with his head bowed. 'Hey, sweet thing,' she said with affection. 'Remember how you came at me like a five-hundred-kilogram Doberman the first time I crawled into your pen? Cole had to jump in front of me to stop you.'

'Jodie.' He stood up straighter then leaned pensively against the fence looking at her like he meant business. Her stomach did another somersault. 'The solicitor said Casper made me executor of the will.'

She blinked at him. 'You?'

'We can schedule a meeting to go over the details but there's something you should know about the inheritance. It's only fair to tell you, too, now that I know myself.'

Jodie stared at him blankly and continued running a hand absently along Mustang's soft mane. She supposed making Cole executor of the will made sense: he'd been like a son to Casper. But she couldn't imagine why she'd inherited anything; she hadn't seen or spoken to her uncle in a long time, aside from the odd Christmas card. Anything to do with him or Everleigh had just reminded her of Cole.

'Jodie, he's left you fifty percent.'

Her hand froze. Surely he couldn't mean what she thought he meant. The estate was worth millions. She made a squeaking noise before her words came out right: 'Fifty percent...of what?'

Cole shook his head, extended his arm and gestured around them. 'This, Jodie. Half of Everleigh, half of the estate.'

Half of the estate? She shook her head numbly. It was a moment before she could speak.

'Well...what about the other half?' she managed, pulling her arms around herself. This was crazy. What would her father say?

Cole took off his hat and dragged a hand through his hair, like he didn't know what to say, and suddenly she knew.

'You?' Jodie almost laughed in shock, and stumbled over a pile of straw.

'Equal shares,' he confirmed, putting a hand on her elbow to steady her. 'This is as much of a surprise to me as it is to you. I thought he'd leave everything to your dad; his only brother.'

Jodie's throat was dry. She buried her face lower into his scarf, struggling to comprehend what was happening. The soft, warm wool smelled like Cole, like comfort and cologne... and pain and rejection.

She crossed to the fence beside him, leaned against it for support. 'This is nuts... I mean, what am I supposed to do here? What does he want me to do with half of Everleigh?'

Cole shrugged. 'Work on it with me?'

'With you?' Jodie almost laughed again. The idea was preposterous. 'Cole, we haven't spoken in the last twelve years; we wouldn't even be speaking now if Casper hadn't died.'

'I know. Jodie, I'm as shocked as you are, but it's what he wanted.'

She shook her head as Mustang snuffled on the hay at their feet. 'Well, he didn't think it through. I have a life in Scotland now, Cole, so I'll have to sell my half.'

'You can't,' he said simply, standing taller and exiting the stall. She stopped at the gate behind him and crossed her arms.

'What do you mean, I can't sell? It's my half. I appreciate it, I really do, it's…life-changing. But I can't work here with you at Everleigh.'

'I know we have history.' He sounded almost regretful now and she felt sick again, just re-membering how many nights she'd cried her-self to sleep waiting for the call from him that had never come. 'We've both done things that hurt the other…'

'What did I do to hurt *you*, exactly?' Jodie was genuinely baffled. He'd left her so broken it had taken months, maybe even years to reas-semble the shattered fragments of her former self. Cole said nothing, his mouth becoming a thin line. It dawned on her what he'd meant.

'Do you mean getting married and having a

baby? Did I hurt you by moving on with my life?' she said incredulously.

Cole eyebrows furrowed. 'It was only six months after we broke up, Jodie.'

She was absolutely furious now. How *dared* he? 'What's timing got to do with it? Your timing wasn't great either, breaking up with me right as we were meant to move to Edinburgh together! You never contacted me again, Cole! You never even told me what had changed between us.'

She reined her emotions back quickly before they could get the better of her. A simmering fury was coursing through her bloodstream as she faced him head on. He had no idea what she'd been through with Ethan either, wearing a ring, walking down the aisle for the whispering media just to appease his father and keep the public in high regard of all his damned political aspirations.

Mustang shuffled a few steps further away, as if sensing a storm brewing. 'I'm definitely selling my share,' she reiterated. 'I can tell you that already.'

Cole pursed his lips at the floor. 'I thought you'd say that.'

Jodie bristled. 'Well, considering our history, can you blame me for not throwing a party?'

He ran a hand across his chin. 'Jodie, Casper had it written into the will that you can't sell your half for a year.'

'What?' She felt like he'd tasered her.

'The will stipulates that you have to come back here as often as you can during that year, a minimum of three days each time. We're to maintain the property and assets together. Then, if after a year, you still want to sell, you're free to do so.'

She shook her head, totally shocked.

'It's what Casper wanted.'

'Th-this is unreal,' she stuttered. 'Why? I mean, why did he want both of us here? This is your home, not mine.'

Cole just shrugged again. 'It was your home too, once.'

Her phone buzzed on silent mode in her pocket. Grateful for the interruption, she swiped to answer it and walked towards the stable exit. Her heart was beating like a drum.

'It's Meg at The Ship Inn,' chirped the voice down the phone. 'Our heating's out, honey. Is there any way you can stay at Everleigh tonight?'

Jodie drew a sharp breath as she heard Cole bolt the gate to Mustang's stall. *What would go wrong next?*

'I don't know if that's a good idea,' she heard herself say. The urge to get as far away from Cole as possible, to process all this new information was imperative if she wasn't going to spontaneously combust, but the wind was howling outside and the snow was settling thick and heavy. Escape was looking less likely with every passing second.

CHAPTER FIVE

'HOW MANY ANIMALS do you see a day?' Emmie asked. She was sitting on his swivel chair in a vivid blue T-shirt. Cole didn't recognise the picture of the band on the front of it.

'About twenty, give or take, between the team,' he told her, lifting the German shepherd's ears one by one and shining the light around the tufts of fur. The dog wasn't scratching like he'd been before, and was much calmer.

'Twenty? That's probably more than my mum sees at West Bow in a day, and she works *all* the time. You know she has her own practice? I'm surprised she's even taking one day off from it. What's wrong with this dog?'

So many questions, he thought in amusement. 'Otitis,' he said.

Emmie raised her eyebrows. 'Sounds like the name of an indie band.'

'It's a pretty common ear infection in dogs, actually.'

Cole hadn't invited Jodie's daughter into the surgery but she'd appeared of her own accord an hour ago. She seemed to be interested in learning about the place and what they did at a countryside veterinary practice.

He didn't mind the company. She seemed like a bright, intelligent kid and it was still strange being here without Casper. He just hoped there wouldn't be any emergencies. The unprecedented amount of snow still falling was punching as many holes in Everleigh's schedule as Casper's sudden absence, and the news about his and Jodie's shared inheritance had shaken him. He hadn't known a thing about Casper's decision till the solicitor had called, and from the look on Jodie's face last night she hadn't expected it either.

'My team usually handles appointments like this,' he told his curious new assistant. 'Dacey's the dermatologist and Vinny's the small animal practitioner. They'll be here soon if they can get through the snow.'

'So, what do *you* do here?'

'A mix of things. I do the house calls for livestock mostly. And the animal therapy.'

'Animal therapy?' Emmie's eyes were as

round and blue as Jodie's, he thought again. He wondered if she knew anything about her mother's former boyfriends, or how uncomfortable Jodie was clearly finding it being back here. Jodie seemed like a great mother, from what he'd seen so far. Last night she'd left him in the stables to find Emmie and tell her they might have to stay a few more days to sort some things out.

When he'd stepped back into the house they'd been chatting by the fire in the kitchen. Emmie had seemed relatively unfazed, whatever her mother had told her, though Jodie had made an effort to stay away from him before the live-in housekeeper, Evie, had shown her to her room.

'What's animal therapy?' Emmie queried now, drumming a pen on the desk. 'Is that... like, emotional support for animals?'

'That's a good way to put it. It's about being part vet, part detective, part therapist. People come to me with their animal problems, and then I help the animals with their people problems. Pass me that stethoscope, will you?'

The door creaked open. 'There you are!' Jodie poked her head in. She visibly tensed in the doorway at the sight of them together. He noticed his bulky black scarf over her arm and couldn't ignore the way his jaw clenched at her sudden appearance.

She'd looked pretty good in his scarf last night, like old times. She'd looked infuriatingly good in the black lace dress too. In fact, Jodie's presence on the estate was undoing him quietly. What with laying Casper to rest, and Jodie unearthing so many other things at the same time, he'd been lucky to catch a couple of hours' sleep before his wake-up call at five a.m. And then there was Blaze's imminent arrival.

'Cole was just telling me about how he's part vet, part detective, part therapist,' Emmie said. 'I saw the manège and the stables when we drove in. Do people bring the big animals here, to you?'

'Depends how big we're talking,' he said with a straight face. 'I haven't seen an elephant in a while.'

'An elephant?'

'We had a lot of those in Sri Lanka.'

'Emmie, Cole's trying to work,' Jodie interjected, one hand still on the door handle. 'Let's go.'

'I don't mind Emmie being here,' he told her.

Cole ran the stethoscope over the German shepherd's chest and ribs in a final check-up before release. When he glanced up, Jodie was watching him as intently as Emmie was. She seemed to remember she was holding his scarf and went about hanging it on a hook on the wall.

It was the wrong place for it now, he thought, appreciating her pert backside in her jeans. He kept it on the hook by the kitchen door, but he wasn't going to tell her that. Her being here, staying in the house, was kind of strange, but he liked the way she was retracing old steps, like the spirit of the Jodie who'd been here before.

She looked good with a few more pounds on her—curves and curls had always been his 'type'. Not that he'd had too many relationships, only Jodie and Diyana in Sri Lanka. He wondered if Jodie would ask him about Sri Lanka.

'How many horses do you have here?' Emmie asked.

'You're into horses, huh?'

'She's mad about horses,' Jodie answered.

'My horse Saxon is seven, we keep him on a farm a few miles from home. Mum used to come riding with us more, but she's usually too busy these days.'

Jodie looked uncomfortable and he detected a small rift for the first time.

He nodded. 'Well, we have eight here already on the estate, and more space than that beyond the gates. You're both welcome to ride while you're here,' he said. 'Kids come in and ride them at weekends. We're on a bit of a hiatus with that now because of our change in circumstances, but seeing as you're here...' He glanced at Jodie before continuing and she looked at him gratefully.

'There's room for more rescues too, when they start coming in,' he added, 'We were working on creating a safe space for mistreated animals.'

Emmie sat up straighter on the chair. 'Here? You'd have a rescue centre here?'

'Sure, why not? It's something your mum and I thought about setting up a long time ago, when we were kids.'

'Really?' Emmie looked thrilled.

'There are a lot of people who own horses who shouldn't, Emmie,' he continued. 'Others have accidents, or they can't live where they used to. Blaze is just one of them. He'll be arriving this morning, so you'll meet him.'

Jodie stepped further into the room. 'Blaze?'

'He was found running loose after a fire took out his enclosure.'

'That's awful. How hurt was he?'

'He's pretty messed up.'

Emmie was looking between them in interest. 'Hey, Emmie, meet me out by the stables in five,' Cole said, seeing the discomfort on Jodie's face. He felt bad for a second. Maybe he shouldn't have mentioned anything they'd planned together once, in front of the child she'd had with another guy, but it was the truth after all. He'd messed up all hopes of him and Jodie setting up the rescue centre here together when he'd broken things off, but if she *was* going to be spending more time here for a while, she'd see him going ahead with it, whether she sold her half eventually or not. There was no way he was stopping now. The horses needed him. He'd made too many promises.

'I have a job for you,' he told Emmie. 'So wrap up warm.'

She pulled a face. 'It's not mucking out, is it?'

'No.'

'Can I ride?'

'Not now.' He took the German shepherd's file and ushered her off the chair. 'Maybe later,' he added, dropping into the seat as she sprang from it. 'We'll all go out if the snow clears. It's better at sunset anyway.'

Emmie slipped past Jodie in the doorway and he slid his coffee flask across the desk, peered inside. *Empty, dammit.*

'Cole?' Jodie had shut the door. She stopped in front of the desk and he studied her boots on the floor tiles. The tension swirled up between them like dust from freshly swept hay as he marked the file and gave the dog the all-clear for pick-up.

'Cole. This rescue centre…'

'It's not fully planned out yet,' he said, putting his pen down. 'You know how things work around here.'

She bit her lip for a second. 'Not any more I don't. You didn't exactly go out of your way to involve me till now.'

He cleared his throat. He supposed he deserved that. 'We thought we'd start with Blaze, see how things go. It could be good for the place in the long term. We finalised the agreements just days before Casper...' He trailed off. Jodie's face softened suddenly.

'I understand, Cole.'

'I couldn't pull out of this after he died, Jodie.'

'I told you, I understand.'

He knew she understood his loyalty to Casper, but he could see the inner conflict at work behind her eyes already. Jodie had decided on the spot to sell her half of the property, right as Blaze was about to arrive and the rescue plan they'd devised together long ago was coming somewhat into fruition.

Would she still sell? He entertained the notion of her changing her mind, then stopped himself. She had spelled it out loud and clear last night. She might not be wearing a wedding ring any more but she had a life in Scotland and a practice of her own, and a daughter settled in school. Why would she want anything to do with Everleigh—or him—any more?

'So, Blaze was running loose?' She rested a butt cheek on the desk, folded her arms.

'A kid found him out on the heath a while ago; he's a skewbald, chestnut and white, but he was almost black from third- and fourth-degree burns. He's lost about fifteen percent of his body weight and he still won't eat.'

'Unbelievable.'

'Someone knew to call me. The horse had no-where to go. The owner doesn't want him back, not in this state, he's traumatised. We've been keeping him up at Honeybrook till his wounds healed enough so he could travel.'

'A skewbald that was almost black,' she echoed, glowering at the floor.

'I promised the kid who found him I'd try my best. I need time. I need him here. I thought the training might be good for me too. Maybe a project like this will help take people's minds off…'

'Losing Casper. I know.'

Cole swallowed back the lump in his throat, picking up the pen and tapping it on the desk to fill the silence. He didn't trust his voice now. Casper's death was the reason Jodie was back here. He'd barely had time to process what it might mean for him, or her, going forward, but he couldn't stop thinking about the night Casper had stopped him going to Jodie, after his father had died. Jodie didn't know; he'd never told her. Only Casper had known.

Twelve years earlier...

Cole took the notebook from his satchel and sat down on the hay bale. Resting it on top of his hardcover copy of Hemingway's *For Whom the Bell Tolls*, he got out his pen and tuned his ears to the soft patter of rain on the corrugated iron.

He'd come to the stables for peace, like he always did when his mind got too loud, but pushing back into the warmth of his hood against the bales he struggled with what to say on paper.

He couldn't call Jodie now, he didn't trust his mouth not to betray him.

He'd known something was different, though, when he'd first walked into the surgery with the backpack and an overnight train ticket, and a vague idea of how to find her when he got to the student campus. The air had felt thicker even before Casper took one look at him and said, 'Don't go to her now. Jodie's pregnant. She met a Scotsman up there, and it seems pretty serious. She's going to marry him.'

Jodie was having some guy's baby at nineteen, just months into vet school? It had to have been a mistake, surely?

But she was *marrying* him...so maybe she

was really in love. He felt bile in his throat at the thought.

Either way, he couldn't go and knock on her door and ask for a second chance now. That would be too much for him to handle. Seeing Jodie like that, with someone else's baby inside her... Hell, no. Maybe he should write down everything he would have said in person, and send it in a letter.

April 15th
Jodie,
What can I say? I was going to come to Edinburgh this weekend to try and talk to you. I wanted to show you how much I love you. I never stopped loving you. I was about to get on the train but Casper told me not to, because you're pregnant and engaged. It feels like I just lost you all over again, this time for ever.

My dad's dead, Jodie. He drowned. They just pulled him out of a river, so he can't hurt you, or us, any more. When he got out of jail I didn't want him getting anywhere near you, or Mum. I guess this is a good time to admit he beat the hell out of me for years before he got locked up for tax evasion. I didn't mean to push you this far away, but I thought I was saving you from the misery of it all.

You saw him drunk that night the police came, and you saw me messed up lots of times, but he did worse things than that. He threatened to hurt the animals, and Mum, and you if I ever told anyone about him.

I told myself when I broke up with you that I was doing the right thing. I thought I was saving you from worrying about me, or getting yourself involved in any of my family's mess. I knew you would confront him and put yourself in danger for me—you're just like that and I love you for it. I wanted you to go and do better things with your life than wait around for me, at least for now. But now you're having a baby!

I wish I'd talked to you about all this before I lost you. Maybe we could have figured something out together. I will always love you and, God, I will miss you, but more than that I want you to be happy.
Yours...

Mustang's soft muzzle against his shoulder brought him back to the moment.

Yours...

Yours what?

Yours for ever? Yours not any more? Yours truly? He'd told her the truth after all. He wondered if she'd guessed *some* of what had been going on in his home, seeing as he'd never taken her back there. Or maybe he'd hidden it so well that this news would be a complete shock, but surely she would understand he'd never wanted to darken her light with the details.

Reading over it again, he realised he could have told her more in the letter, like how all the cuts on his neck that time weren't from crawling under barbed wire, chasing a chicken, like he'd said, but from blocking the glass table after his father had hurled it at him from across the living room.

There had been countless times he'd lied to Jodie to protect her. Pretending to her that he hadn't wanted her in his life any more had been only one of them, even if it had been the biggest lie of all.

A dog's bark told him someone was passing the kennels. Cole gathered his hat and the notebook, and halfway towards the house he decided he wouldn't send the letter. It wasn't fair to do it now she'd found happiness with someone else.

Over dinner he changed his mind.

In the morning, he sealed the letter with an old-fashioned wax stamp in Casper's study. It looked final, meaningful...ominous.

Kicking his boots up on the desk he wielded the pen and then realised he didn't have an address. He *would* send it...but he'd have to get the exact address from Casper first.

One week later, he slipped the unaddressed envelope into a box, where the sight of it couldn't cause his stomach to twist into knots. What would a pregnant woman do with that information anyway? What right did he have to contact Jodie with his excuses now that she was happy, with a good man taking care of her? He should have told her sooner, instead of being such a coward.

She hadn't contacted him herself anyway, and she would have heard about his father by now, surely. She probably wanted nothing more to do with him.

Weeks turned into months and the excuses kept on coming, until eventually the letter went nowhere, and Cole went on with his life without Jodie.

'Have you ever worked a snow blower before?' Cole asked Emmie, wheeling the giant lawn-mower-type machine from the shed onto the snowy gravel.

'Not exactly.'

'Well, it's as good a time as any to learn. We need this pathway clear before Blaze arrives. We have other clients who'll need to get in with their animals, too. It's a pretty important job, are you up for it?'

Emmie shrugged, pushing her freshly brushed hair over her shoulder. 'I don't know. Maybe.'

'Less enthusiasm, please. We try to keep things cool around here,' he teased, and Jodie watched as Emmie bit back a smile.

It was interesting, watching their interactions. Emmie was sometimes difficult, but he seemed to know instinctively how to handle her. She supposed his intuition was a big part of what had clearly made him so successful. Casper's financial help had been a boost, but no more than strapping a firework onto a rocket ship.

She wondered if he'd ever thought about having kids of his own, or whether he'd met anyone else after their break-up. She hadn't asked him anything about his life after her. She hadn't exactly had much time yet, but then again she almost didn't want to know. She was emotional enough already and sleep hadn't come for her last night till well after three a.m.

Damn Cole for looking so sexy, she thought yet again as he yanked the starter motor and the snow blower spluttered to life in front of them. He tossed her his coffee flask and put a gloved hand over Emmie's to guide her as she started to wheel the juddering machine over the thick white snow that had piled up by the stable entrance. 'Finish up around here, then you can start around the cabin, yes?'

'Yes, sir, whatever you say.' Emmie mock saluted him, but Jodie could tell she was enjoying herself. Together they watched her set off up the path, blowing snow happily into smaller piles at the sides of the road.

'A woman on a mission,' she commented, mostly to herself.

'I can see where she gets that from.' Cole grinned. 'If she wants to ride later, she'll work for it, like *we* both had to.'

Jodie stifled a laugh, even as discomfort settled in at his proximity now they were alone. Usually she'd be concerned about her daughter operating machinery she'd never used, but Cole oozed confidence in everything he did and it seemed to be rubbing off on Emmie like it had her once.

There was something about Everleigh that had always made her feel quite safe. Good energy in the air, she realised, even though Casper wasn't here. It didn't mean she'd be uprooting herself to make a base here, though. Far from it.

They'd be meeting with the solicitor, Ms Tanner, as soon as she could make it to discuss the options. Jodie was hoping there would be a way around the caveat. Coming all the way back down here so often, as Casper had stipulated, would be hugely inconvenient for everyone, especially Emmie.

And me, she thought, eyeing Cole.

Her insides shifted, thinking about the rescue

horse and his plans for starting a rescue centre here. The horses needed Cole and his own special way of dealing with their physical and emotional needs. If she sold her share to someone else, they might not have as much enthusiasm for his...methods. They wouldn't have a clue what Everleigh meant to him either.

Not your problem, she reminded herself.

'Casper made you work for everything,' Cole remembered out loud, catching her eye from under another woolly hat and taking the coffee flask she'd forgotten she was holding. 'You hated it at first, but you still got up at five a.m. when there was something important to do.'

'The coffee always helped,' she admitted as Emmie shrieked in delight again up ahead.

'Black, no milk, no sugar.'

'I'm surprised you remember how I like my coffee,' she replied. 'It seemed a lot to me like you wanted to forget everything about me.'

He shook his head slowly. From the corner of her eye she saw him scuff one boot into the snow, disgruntled. 'I gave you the wrong impression then. I do regret that, Jodie. I regret a lot of things from back then. I was sorry to hear you got divorced.'

Jodie bristled. She'd been after some kind of explanation as to why he'd changed his mind about her, and Edinburgh, not to hear him admit he'd felt sorry for her circumstances after sending her off, albeit unwittingly, into a marriage she and Ethan had both known would be over before Emmie had even reached her teens.

'It was never going to last for ever,' she admitted quietly. 'Me and Ethan.'

He raised an eyebrow in interest. 'Casper said you got divorced right after you graduated.'

She kept her head high. She didn't want his pity and she certainly didn't owe him any explanations about the quiet untethering she and Ethan had agreed to once they'd both completed their studies successfully and all prying eyes had stopped paying much attention. But it wasn't like Ethan's name wouldn't keep coming up.

'That's right, we did. We decided we were much better as friends.'

She couldn't read him, but she continued matter-of-factly, 'We're a good team, you know? We make everything work for Emmie. They spend a lot of time together with Saxon, her horse. Ethan's as mad about horses as you.'

'Is that right?' Cole's lips curved. She thought he looked smug. They both knew that probably wasn't true.

She realised her heart had quickened under her ribs. 'Emmie doesn't know about us. You and me, I never told her about our history, Cole. I haven't tried to hide anything but at the same time I didn't think she needed to know. She hasn't been herself lately, since Ethan moved in with Saskia. I think she's still processing it.'

Cole held his hands up. 'She won't hear anything from me.'

Jodie let the pent-up air leave her mouth. She probably shouldn't even care, but it *was* her duty to protect Emmie from any information that might make her feel awkward while they were here. She hadn't mentioned the inheritance to her yet, let alone any of the 'rules' Casper had made.

A tall, skinny kid in a flat cap, thick black-rimmed glasses and bright blue welly boots wandered out from the storeroom. He'd been talking to Emmie at the funeral. 'Cole, I'm done with the dog food delivery, it's all stacked up. What else can I do?'

Cole pointed with his flask at Emmie. 'Can

you help Emmie over there with the snow blower?'

'Sure thing. Oh, hi, Ms Everleigh, I saw you yesterday in the house. I'm Toby. The kid held out a hand to her and Jodie shook it in mild amusement before he set off purposefully up the path after Emmie.

'Toby lives up at Forster's Nursery,' Cole explained. 'He started showing up every day last summer to help out in the kennels. He walks and feeds the dogs, and we let him ride the horses.'

'Sounds like a fair trade.' It hadn't escaped her attention the way Cole was handling everything here so stoically, knowing he was grieving for Casper. Then again, he'd always been good at keeping his emotions in check— even when he'd broken up with her, he hadn't flinched. Had he ever really loved her?

'He's here most weekends and holidays,' he told her, picking up a thick black hose off the ground and coiling it around his arm. 'Keeps him out of trouble while school's out. He loves his school.'

'Nice for Toby. Emmie stays with her dad most holidays, or with her friend Claire. We go riding with Saxon together sometimes…when I have time.'

'You can bring Saxon here when you come,' Cole offered.

'That might be nice,' she admitted. 'I'm not sure what Ethan would think about that, though. He loves that horse as much as Emmie.'

Cole's jaw was spasming now. She thought for a second he was going to say something else about how her busy schedule might impinge on the requirements of Casper's will because she was already thinking it herself. But he didn't.

'He sounds like a great father.'

'He is.'

Cole looked like he was about to ask her something else but his phone pinged. He looped the heavy hose over its hook on the stable wall as if it weighed nothing. As he talked on the phone she studied the shape of him, the way his shoulders had broadened and his muscles filled out. She found herself remembering a water fight right here that had dissolved into furious lovemaking. Her cheeks reddened. *So many memories.*

'Do you want the good news or the bad news?' Cole asked, sliding his phone back into his jeans pocket and running a hand across his beard.

Jodie pulled a face at him. 'The good news?'

'The Ship Inn's heating system is fixed. Your rooms are ready if you still want them. I can drive you up there later as Barry still needs a part for your car. The way it is, I wouldn't trust it to get you very far.'

'Thanks,' she said, wondering who the heck Barry was. Cole knew so many people. She hadn't even realised he had taken it on himself to get her car fixed already, but she was grateful. 'What's the bad news?'

'The solicitor left a message. Her daughter picked up some bug and she needs to stay home with her a bit longer.'

Jodie frowned.

'We can reschedule,' Cole said, shrugging.

She tried not to look like she was unravelling. 'I have to get Emmie home for school, and I'm due back at West Bow on Monday.'

Emmie emitted another shriek of laughter in the distance, and Toby's own voice travelled indistinguishably up the driveway. Their happiness didn't match her mood. This messed up her whole schedule.

She followed a silent Cole into the stables. 'I guess I could still leave, and we could have the meeting on the phone,' she started, watching him pull two pitchforks from their hooks on the wall. 'But, then, what if we need to sign papers? I don't know, Cole, I think we should both be present for this. I've come all the way here.' She turned for the door. 'I'll go and make some calls...'

'Jodie,' he said calmly, catching her elbow. 'There's nothing we can do about any of this now.' He held out one of the pitchforks. 'Let's just focus on Blaze. He's going to need us.'

CHAPTER SIX

COLE HAD RATHER enjoyed the sight of Jodie wielding the pitchfork in the hay in the stalls, shoving her hair behind her ears every ten seconds and trying to look like she still enjoyed getting this dirty.

She was watching him now from outside the horse trailer, standing on the snow-free gravel, keeping both Toby and Emmie at a safe distance. Cole and Russell, his stablehand, were attempting to move Blaze out of the trailer into the outdoor enclosure, but so far he wasn't budging.

'He's extra fired up after being in here,' he called back to Jodie. 'Stay well back, all of you.'

He slid around to the side of the trailer with his back flat to the wall. He had to move slowly so the horse would know he didn't pose a threat. But Blaze seemed to be going out of his way not to make his job easy and kept shuffling away from his eye contact.

'You've met me before, boy.' He offered a chunk of apple as a peace offering. The horse refused to so much as sniff it.

Cole stood stock still, studying the deep, black flesh wounds around Blaze's left eye socket. He was on meds, but still losing weight after the barn fire. His ribs were almost jutting through the flesh and the horse was a whirlwind of emotions. Cole could almost see the tension rippling through every muscle. 'What you must have been through, buddy...'

He saw it coming half a second before it happened. With a wild sound the horse reared up and almost slammed his own head on the trailer roof.

'Watch out!' Russell leapt from the back doors to the ground to avoid being kicked, leaving Blaze's reins swinging.

'Enough,' Cole ordered, reaching for the reins. Blaze was too fast. The horse startled back, whinnying in fear, and darted from the trailer half a second before Cole could reach him. As he watched, Jodie urged the kids away and moved towards Blaze.

'Jodie, move!' Cole was on the ground now. 'What are you doing?'

Blaze bypassed the gate to the enclosure and reared up again, right in front of Jodie. 'It's OK,' she said, holding out a hand.

'Mum!' Emmie looked panicked, and Jodie made a valiant grab for the reins before Cole skidded across a freshly iced-over patch of grass and yanked her away, shielding her with his own body.

'Don't move,' he told her, one arm wrapped tightly around her heaving chest, beneath her breasts. He held the other up at Blaze, who snorted indignantly. If Cole hadn't stood six feet two, the horse might have attempted to jump over his head; Blaze looked determined as hell.

'I almost had it,' Jodie panted indignantly when he released her. She hurried to Emmie behind the enclosure and Cole cracked his long leather lash on the ground in front of Blaze's forelegs, forcing the horse backwards into the enclosure before he could lunge again. Russell was quick on his feet. He slammed the gate shut behind them.

'Better we just have me in here for now, Russ,' Cole told him, checking Jodie was safe behind the fence. 'Can you go prep the stall, make sure the others are calm when we bring him in?'

'His face,' Emmie said in horror. He had to agree Blaze's injuries looked bad. He was scuffing at the ground with one bandaged hoof then the other. His red-raw ears were pointed high and alert. His blackened nose twitched as he snorted at them both, swishing what was left of his thick brown tail.

Cole knew the horse felt cornered and defensive, and both he and Blaze loathed the lash, but right now it was necessary for everyone's safety.

'The poor thing,' he heard Emmie say. 'He looks so…scared.'

Blaze started snorting in fury, giving him a look like he was going to charge. Cole cracked the lash on the ground at his side, whipping up the snow.

'Mum, what's he doing?'

'It's OK, Emmie, Cole's just showing Blaze who's in control.'

'But he's hurt!'

'He needs to learn some respect. Cole can only help him if they can trust each other.'

Cole got to his knees in the snow, a metre from Blaze, half listening to Jodie. The way she was explaining things to Emmie was just like how Casper used to speak to her back when she'd known nothing about horses.

He sat there in silence, letting Blaze know he wasn't moving, but wasn't there to harm him either. The horse was starting to understand.

'When Mustang first arrived, Cole sat there for three hours in a face-off. He had to wait till Mustang came to *him*,' Jodie explained quietly.

'He'll look like a snowman soon if neither of them moves,' Emmie replied, though Cole hadn't really noticed the snowflakes settling on his jacket. He was trying to stay still and maintain eye contact with Blaze.

Eventually, after what felt like a long time, Blaze walked tentatively forward and nuzzled his hat. 'There you go,' he said calmly, placing a hand gently on the horse's forelock. 'Are you OK with this?'

The horse met his eyes, and finally Cole was able to stroke around the burns on his face without the animal startling. He murmured in reassurance.

'How did he do that?' Emmie sounded incredulous as they watched Cole mount Blaze and canter around the circumference of the en-

closure, the horse kicking up the snow as the driver of the trailer rattled off up the pathway.

'It's just what Cole does, sweetheart,' Jodie replied. 'It's what makes him…'

Cole heard her pause. He knew she'd been about to say something like 'special' but had stopped herself.

'I think Blaze knows no more harm will come to him here,' he said, exchanging a look with Jodie on his walk over to the fence. 'He's OK, but he's still a little apprehensive. We can't blame him.'

'He's just like Mustang used to be, so I know you'll get there,' she told him, putting a reassuring hand on his shoulder before removing it and looking away.

He nodded thoughtfully, his thoughts focused solely on Blaze again. He had a big job ahead of him with this one. Jodie knew as well as he did that connecting with this horse enough to help him make a full emotional and physical recovery was going to take time.

There was so much to do in Casper's absence. The last thing he needed was for some other buyer to come in and change the way they'd always done things. If Jodie sold her share, changes were imminent. The thought made his breath catch in his chest. He didn't like change. Only the two of *them* knew how Casper had worked, and the faith he'd had in Cole.

'Are we leaving him in here?' Emmie asked, looking between them.

'For now,' he replied, realising his eyes were fixed on the blush of Jodie's cheeks. 'We'll put him inside when he's calmer.'

'Can we give him a reward for backing down?' The kids both looked like they were about to climb on the fence to try and give Blaze more treats he probably wouldn't eat.

Jodie stepped in before he could. 'Give him space,' she warned them. 'Leaving Blaze alone is the greatest reward we can give him for now.'

'Dinner!'

The call from the porch sent the kids running.

'It's *we* now, is it?' Cole remarked, once it was just him and Jodie standing there. He brushed the snow from his hat and drew the double bolt across the gate, fighting back a smile as she pulled a face and shrugged.

This was the Jodie he'd known before. In spite of everything they'd been through in the years apart from each other, Cole felt mild relief to see *some* things hadn't changed.

'So how long are we staying here now, Mum?' Emmie asked.

'I'm not sure yet,' she said. 'I'm sorry, sweetie. We might have to take you out of school for a few days this week.'

Emmie grinned. 'I don't mind. I mean, about school. I do miss Saxon, but Toby says there's a litter of puppies here due any day. We can help look after them and then we can find them new homes. And Cole says I can go for a ride on Mustang.'

Jodie watched Emmie's face light up in the glow of the fire from the pit. 'Did he now?'

She had expected a different reaction to the news that they had to stay a couple more days, but first Cole and now Toby seemed to be swaying her city-loving daughter in favour of country life.

'I like Cole,' Emmie said suddenly.

Jodie felt adrenaline spike as Ziggy laid his soft head across her boots on the gravel. She was slowly processing the fact that she'd inherited half of everything Cole and Casper had been working on in her absence. But she hadn't been prepared for the way just looking at Cole made her feel every time he walked into a room.

His gravitational pull was just as strong as it ever had been, but he was also a grown-man-sized reminder of the heartache she'd suffered over him. She couldn't think why Casper would make it so she had to spend all this extra time here when he must have known it would open Pandora's box. Was he laughing about this somewhere up in heaven?

The sooner she could discuss her options with the solicitor the better.

'I like the way he's so good with the horses,' Emmie continued, just as Cole's broad silhouette appeared before the warmly lit cabin and he made his way over. 'And I'm learning a lot more here than I would at school. I just made a fire. I sent a photo to Dad while you were in the house, look!'

Emmie thrust her phone at Jodie, and Jodie got a glimpse of the snap. Emmie and Cole together, holding up chunks of wood, both of them grinning like they'd felled the tree themselves.

'You sent that photo somewhere?' Cole asked in interest over Jodie' shoulder.

'To my dad.'

Cole's eyes flickered towards Jodie as he took his seat at the firepit. The centre of the ring was ablaze after he'd sent Emmie to gather wood from the shed, and taught her how to start the fire carefully and slowly without sending a cloud of black smoke billowing across the estate.

Cole knew she hadn't told Emmie about their romantic history, so of course Emmie wouldn't think twice about sending Ethan a photo of them together. Ethan knew where she was, of course. She'd told him she was going to have a reunion with the guy she'd been trying to get over all those years ago when they'd met at college—he'd even wished her luck.

But she hadn't told him why they were staying a few more days, exactly. She wanted the chance to discuss this inheritance and the terms of the will with him in person. It would involve him, either way, because if she had to be down in Dorset more, he would have to consent to having Emmie more often when he'd only just moved in with Saskia. She couldn't have her missing a lot more school.

Cole placed a bag of marshmallows on the ground and handed her a wooden-handled toasting fork.

'For old times' sake,' he said, and she raised an eyebrow. She had no interest in doing anything for old times' sake with Cole, not that she could stop the barrage of memories flying at her unannounced, like hungry birds. It wasn't particularly difficult to conjure up the sweaty, stormy nights they'd spent locked in each other's arms, but it also wasn't too hard to recall throwing up in the bathroom of the train station after he'd told her it was over. She'd half assumed he'd roll up and apologise, or change his mind, and she'd waited for him so long on the platform she'd let three trains go by before finally getting on one.

Still, she wasn't about to show hostility towards the man with Emmie here.

'Crispy on the outside, runny in the middle,' Jodie heard him say to Emmie, quoting what Casper had always said. 'Stuffed between two biscuits. That's the way to do it.'

'With a gourmet chocolate flourish,' she mumbled without thinking.

She realised Emmie was looking between them quizzically now. 'How long did you say you've known each other?'

'A very long time,' Cole answered as Jodie ran a hand through her hair, feeling frazzled.

'How come I've never heard about you before?'

'Maybe I'm just not that interesting.' With a wink Cole crouched down beside Emmie and pierced a marshmallow hard straight from the packet with his fork. 'Are you ready for the Everleigh delicacy? We call these s'mores. It's an American recipe, if you can call it a recipe, but they taste just as good here. Hold your marshmallow above the fire, not in it…like that…yes.'

Thankfully Emmie seemed to forget her probing questions and soon lost herself in the art of making s'mores with Cole. Jodie wasn't sure what to make of the fact that Emmie seemed to be forming a bond with him already.

Her eyes found the old scar on the back of Cole's neck as he leaned over the fire with his stick. He'd got cut as a kid, crawling under barbed wireas he went after an escaped chicken. She hadn't seen him do it, but she'd seen the way it'd bled through the plasters. She'd had to help him change them, more than once.

'Maybe I can help with the other horses while you're training Blaze,' she heard Emmie say to Cole. 'Mum always says I should stop being so amazing and try being useful, too.'

Cole let out a snort that turned into a laugh.

'Emmie knows she has to work for her rides,' Jodie explained quickly, shifting in discomfort. He was putting her on edge, being nice to her daughter when Emmie had no clue about their history. She couldn't exactly tell her eleven-year-old she'd still been heartbroken over Cole when she'd slept with her father.

'If we need to stay after tomorrow I can organise more nights at The Ship Inn...'

'Fine by me.' Cole shrugged. 'But there's plenty of room here, too.'

'I'll have to see if the locum can cover for me,' she said. 'I'm running a staff of five but there's a surgery on a beagle I'm supposed to be doing with Aileen...' Jodie stopped, realising she was blabbering.

'Everyone there loves you, Mum. You know

Aileen will be fine with someone else,' Emmie pleaded. 'It makes sense to stay here at the house too. We already have all our stuff with us.'

Jodie was defeated. She studied Cole surreptitiously in the firelight as she ate her first s'more. She really liked his beard the more she looked at his face. She supposed it was also nice that he was so intent on showing Emmie the exact right way to squish the hot, runny marshmallow over the chocolate.

'Mmm-mmm.' Emmie rolled her eyes back dramatically, chewing her own first heavenly bite. 'Where have these been all my life?'

'You look like your mum did when she had her first s'more,' Cole told her, before taking a bite of a lone marshmallow and chewing slowly, purposefully. He held Jodie's gaze, like he was reminding her how his mouth could move…as if she didn't vividly remember. She groaned internally.

They'd spent so many nights here, that summer they'd first kissed, melting into each other's minds, and mouths. They'd had a competition one night to see how many marshmallows they could toast at once, and they'd almost set themselves on fire.

Jodie had asked to go back to his house with him that night, seeing that she'd never stepped foot beyond the gates of Thistles. She was curious by then about what his home life was like. He'd refused to let her, she remembered now. It was the same night they'd had their first argument.

'What was it you used to say?' Cole was gesturing at her with his fork. 'The s'more you're here, the s'more I love the summers.'

She realised she was frowning over all the puzzle pieces of Cole. 'I love you a little s'more every day,' she followed anyway.

'My love for you is s'more than I can handle.' Cole admired his marshmallow as he said it.

'The s'more I eat, the s'more I want,' Emmie joined in, chomping into a biscuit.

Jodie hoped she didn't look as torn as she felt. She hadn't meant them all to get so cosy like this. She'd had every intention of avoiding Cole as much as possible but with Blaze's arrival and the cancelled meeting...and the broken-down car...and the way Cole did that thing to her heartbeat, like pushing a fast-forward button in spite of his reserve. Cole had kept a lot inside as a kid, that much she'd always known. But she'd always felt special when he'd focused on her and forgotten the mask he'd worn for other people. Maybe that's how Emmie felt now.

What was she supposed to do?

CHAPTER SEVEN

THE SNOW WAS MELTING, the horses seemed calm, even the kennels were quiet as Cole crossed the sodden grass in the dark and let himself into the main house.

It was just after five a.m. His head was busy crafting a to-do list for the day as he grabbed a packet of ground coffee from the pantry.

Hickory Farm for the sick lamb... Check up on Rob's heifer... Blaze's first vital stats check—if I can even get close to Blaze today...

'Cole?'

Jodie was standing in the kitchen doorway, drawing a thick pink dressing gown around her, scraping her hair back from her forehead in embarrassment. She clearly hadn't expected to see him either. He noticed she was holding an old copy of *The Wizard of Oz*. It had always been her favourite. Something about the characters finding their courage had appealed to her. It didn't sit well with him to this day.

He smiled, holding up the coffee. 'I ran out, but there's always spare coffee here.'

'Good to know.'

He couldn't keep his eyes off her figure in the dressing gown, her messed-up hair and sleepy eyes. He hadn't seen her just-out-of-bed look in a long time, but it seemed to be affecting him just the same. He ached to get out of there, but he was glued to the floor now. 'Why are you up?'

'I couldn't get back to sleep. It's too quiet here. Thought I'd make some coffee, catch up on some reading.'

'Too quiet, hmm? Maybe your mind is just noisy, like mine.'

She tightened the belt on the dressing gown, blocking his view of her cleavage. 'Since when? You're the calmest person I've ever known.'

'Not since you showed up, Jodie.'

Jodie blinked. Colour flared visibly in her cheeks as she stared at him with her mouth slightly open, like she didn't know what to say. Suddenly he didn't either. He didn't even know why he'd admitted that—it was too early, he wasn't thinking straight yet.

'Seeing as you're awake, get dressed and meet

me at the cabin,' he grunted, before he could change his mind.

It took her less than twenty minutes to knock on his door. She'd dressed in grey jeans and the same boots, which were appropriately muddy now after treading through muck and snow. She was clutching her coffee flask like old times.

'There's a lamb with a swollen face at Hickory Farm, I need to check it out,' he said as she stepped over the threshold. He regretted that he'd just admitted that her presence here was rattling him. He supposed he'd have to get used to it, but the sight of her in that dressing gown…

'Nice place,' she commented, following him through to the kitchen.

'I like it.'

Luckily the cabin was relatively clean and tidy, apart from Ziggy's toys scattered around the fireplace and couch. And the plates and cutlery in the sink…and the messy home 'office' in the corner where he'd recently dismantled a broken printer.

The sound of her boots on the floorboards made his insides twist with some long-dormant memory. Jodie, aged eighteen, dancing around her room in the main house in nothing but her boots and underwear. Just for him.

'Remember Liam Grainger?' he asked, lifting a jumble of jackets and computer cables on the bench and locating his own coffee flask. The pot was ready on the counter top.

'That big old farmer who always had all the holes in his jumper, and the bright red face?' Jodie had stopped by the kitchen door, and was studying the photos on the wall around the giant chicken-shaped clock. She seemed to pause a second by the one of him and Diyana on their elephant.

'That's the guy. Liam will get a kick out of seeing you at Hickory again. Emmie will be fine here with Evie while we're gone. Pass me your flask.'

She held it out without looking at him. She was still studying the photo. 'Is that Sri Lanka?' she asked, eventually.

Cole poured them fresh, hot coffee. 'Yes, that's Sri Lanka. That was our elephant, Khalua. We rescued her from a temple in the Ancient Cities—she was about to be culled instead of retired.'

'She's beautiful.'

'She has a temperament to match. I'd never seen an elephant cry before I saw Khalua in those chains. The tears started pouring from both her eyes the last time we left her in the temple. We knew we had to go back for her.'

'*We?*' Jodie was still looking at the photo. 'You mean…you and this woman?'

'Her name's Diyana,' he said, screwing the lids on both flasks, maybe a little too tightly.

'You had an elephant together?'

He shrugged. 'It was too soon for a baby.'

Jodie's lips became a thin line. Cole immediately regretted his words but he had no clue why Jodie had felt the need to get married so young in the first place. Ethan was a staple in her life still, and a great father, that much he knew, but he was burning with more questions he knew he had no right to ask. All this curiosity over the photo was flicking his triggers.

He'd met Diyana during a summer break long after Jodie had walked down the aisle with Ethan. Diyana had been a welcome distraction, like sticking a plaster over a wound. She'd been interesting and new and she'd taken his mind off Jodie for a while.

'I spent a couple of summers in Sri Lanka

between studies. Casper said it was important to see other places, see more of the world and its creatures, great and small,' he said. 'I heard about a rescue centre for giant flying squirrels in the hill country. Diyana was one of the volunteers. She introduced me to some of the best vets, technicians, researchers... I helped where I could. I travelled around with them. I learned a lot from the animals there. And the people.'

Jodie was looking out of the window. Dawn was starting to break outside and Russell was pushing a giant green wheelbarrow loaded with tools out of the outhouse. 'Was it serious with Diyana?' she asked quietly.

There it was. The green-eyed monster. Cole was well acquainted with this beast. He flipped the lid on his flask, took a sip, letting the hot liquid scald his tongue for a second. 'I came back here without her,' he offered quietly. 'And she isn't here now.'

He almost told her exactly why Diyana wasn't here now. He had no doubt she would have come if he'd asked her to. But he couldn't give her the ring and the happy family she wanted, even after all the time they'd spent dating, because the whole time they'd been together he'd never quite managed to push Jodie out of his head, even if she'd had no difficulty forgetting him.

'Why did you come back to Dorset if you had so much going on elsewhere in the world?' she asked him suddenly. 'You could have gone anywhere, Casper would have still supported your decision.'

'This will always be my home, Jodie. I never wanted to be anywhere else. Ziggy, come, let's go.' He signalled to the dog, then swiped up his car keys from the counter before they could start another discussion about their pasts or their romantic lives that he really didn't have the time or inclination to continue.

Jodie put her hand on the door before he could open it. Her gaze sharpened on his face.

'You're worried I'm going to sell my half of your home, aren't you?'

His heart felt like she'd tugged on it.

He studied her a moment. Her eyes were still like oceans, luring him in, threatening to drown him. Of course he was worried about someone else coming in, but he was more concerned that one of the reasons Jodie was planning on selling was just so she could stay away from him.

'Like I said before, this is your home too,' he said coolly, pulling his plaid jacket from its hook.

'I was never invested in this place as much as you were, Cole.'

'You wanted the rescue centre as much as me,' he said, shrugging on the jacket. It was true and she knew it.

She faltered a second. 'Maybe…once. When we were happy here together. But my home is in Edinburgh now. Ethan is there… Emmie's school is there.'

He turned his back to the door, facing her. She was wearing the too-clean jeans again, another reminder of her city-girl life; a life that wasn't here. 'So you're happy up there in Scotland? Logistics aside, are you so happy you'd never even consider being anywhere else, even part time?'

Jodie tilted her chin, meeting his eyes dead on. 'I don't know why you're suddenly so concerned about my happiness, Cole.'

'Look,' he said, keeping his emotions in check and his voice level. 'I know you want to sell because of me, because of our history.'

'Can you blame me?'

He sighed sharply through his nose. 'No. But Casper wanted us to do something together when he put Everleigh in our hands. Maybe the rescue centre was it, we were always on the same page about that.'

Jodie's voice was indignant. 'I thought we were on the same page about a lot of things, Cole. Turned out I was wrong.'

He opened his mouth to counter her, but what could he say? It was sounding more and more like he'd tainted her whole view of Everleigh when he'd broken things off. She'd loved it because she'd loved him, and now…she despised him.

Jodie pulled the door open, sending a flood of light into the cabin and releasing a pent-up, eager Ziggy, who bolted for the Land Rover. 'It doesn't matter now,' she muttered in annoyance, following his dog. 'Let's just get through this. We should go. The sun's coming up.'

'It's either a blocked saliva gland or she's got some kind of infection,' Cole said. 'I think it's an infection.'

'I trust your instincts by now, Crawford.' Liam Grainger still had the same pot belly and ruddy cheeks Jodie had known before. He was standing with his arms folded behind the wooden fence, observing Cole in action. 'I have to say it sure is nice to see you two together again. How long are you sticking around Everleigh, Jodie?'

'I'm not sure yet,' Jodie told him. 'I have some business to care of at the estate.' She glanced at Cole. '*We* have some business to take care of.'

The bleating of the sheep and other lambs was a symphony all around them. Jodie was still wrestling to keep her mind on the situation at hand, and not on their heated words back at the cabin, or the photo of Cole's beautiful ex-girlfriend riding the elephant with him in Sri Lanka. Maybe that's what had riled her up, more than the terms of Casper's will or Cole's expectations of *her* after all this time.

Every time they talked about anything remotely involving the past, they ended up having some kind of disagreement. Of course he was a big factor in her wanting to leave and sell her share of Everleigh…he wasn't about to guilt her into keeping it just to stop someone else moving in on his precious rescue centre plans.

But seeing that photo framed on the wall had

made her feel quite nauseous. And the dig he'd made when she'd let on her surprise at their elephant: *'It was too soon for a baby.'*

That had been unexpected.

If he was jealous in any way of her relationship with Ethan, he only had himself to blame, she thought angrily, watching him now. He looked impossibly handsome with the sun on his face, carrying a cute lamb into an empty pen. Damn him.

'Ziggy, give that bag to Jodie, buddy.' Cole held a gloved hand out, motioning for the bag Ziggy was still holding in his teeth.

To Jodie's surprise, the dog let go of the bag right at her feet. Jodie let herself into the pen with it, losing her boots in the muck and hay almost instantly.

Cole positioned the tiny lamb's head between his steady thighs to hold her in place. The little thing had been bleating and writhing in the hay in fear when they'd first arrived, but he'd managed to calm her significantly.

The syringe didn't look pretty when he pulled it out. 'It's filled with infection,' Jodie observed, crouching down in the hay and straw and locating a set of scalpels from Cole's bag. She already knew he'd have to put a nick in the swelling to release the rest of the fluid.

Liam Grainger watched them intently from the fence, petting Ziggy from time to time. 'So, why did you stay away so long, Jodie? This place was always more interesting when you two were running around together.'

'I run a private veterinary practice in Edinburgh now,' she told him, holding up a gleaming 'Everleigh' engraved scalpel.

'And you have a husband and a daughter,' Liam said, as though he was only just remembering. 'I guess life gets in the way, huh?'

'Actually, Mr Grainger, I'm not married any more,' she replied with a tight smile.

Liam wriggled his eyebrows mischievously. 'Is that so? Did you tell her you're single too, Crawford? How long's it been now? We keep telling him he needs to find himself a good woman. The man can't cook to save his life.'

'I wouldn't be looking to Jodie to cook for me, Liam,' Cole said dryly. 'Scalpel, please.'

Jodie handed it over, noting the curve of a smile on his lips at his joke—not that it was a joke. She was absolutely awful at cooking. But even the familiar holes in the elbows of Liam's jumper and the fabric that was struggling to contain his ample girth wasn't causing her as much amusement as it should have been. She had a feeling Cole knew she'd been bitten by the green-eyed monster too, over seeing that photo of his ex. She couldn't un-see it now.

Diyana was clearly from Sri Lanka herself. She had a stunning veil of wavy jet-black hair the same shade as Cole's. Her bright pink sari and wide, warm, infectious smile hinted at a woman who loved life. Cole had looked magnificent sitting on the elephant behind her, his muscled arms wrapped tightly around her waist in a linen shirt she'd never seen him wear on any English farm. He'd been in a different world with Diyana. Had he *loved* her?

'Jodie, the alcohol, please?' Cole prompted now, looking up from the lamb's swollen cheek. Jodie was already unscrewing the lid from the plastic container. 'You want to do it?' he asked her.

'Of course,' she said, maintaining her professional stance as best she could. She was somewhat surprised at how she was working on autopilot alongside him. Cole seemed to be calming the jittery lamb with his usual skill and inexplicable aplomb as she took the moment of stillness to douse the fresh wound around the incision and prep another syringe from the bag with a painkiller.

Why hadn't Diyana come back to Everleigh with him? Maybe she wouldn't have liked his cabin as much as Cole did, or as much as she herself did, she mused as they worked. Maybe the piles of papers and jackets and computer parts she'd seen about the place would have driven the poor woman mad.

In spite of his calm and cool demeanour Cole had always lived in organised chaos. The mess had always been refreshing to her as she'd been growing up. Her mother had kept a clean and tidy home in Greenwich, and Jodie had never been allowed to leave anything lying around. At Everleigh, as long as the animals were fed and happy, Casper and Cole didn't care how many dishes were in the farmhouse sink or how many jackets were lying around off their hooks.

Back then, when their friendship had morphed into love, she'd never dreamed she'd ever see Cole Crawford with another woman. But, then, she hadn't exactly pictured herself married with a child at nineteen either.

Emmie seemed to like Cole a lot, and Jodie had no doubt her daughter would love coming to Everleigh more often. Frowning into her scarf, she realised she was using her daughter and Ethan as an excuse for keeping away, and for selling up, when she and Cole both knew she was only reluctant to be here because of him. He'd said it himself.

'She'll be fine without the antibiotics, Liam,' Cole said now, standing up tall and allowing the lamb to wriggle free. 'She's much more comfortable now the fluid is all out. See how she's bouncing around? She'll be eating again before you know it, you can't keep creatures like this down.'

Cole opened the gate and let Jodie exit the stall first. As he went about packing the equipment up, Jodie watched the little lamb cross on wobbly legs to the corner of the stall, where a fresh batch of straw was tied to the wooden fencing.

As it began munching on the hay with renewed interest, Jodie shook her head at Liam without Cole seeing. She would always be amazed at the way animals seemed to respond to his quiet handling, and how well he could predict and relate to them. She'd met a lot of great vets in her time but, God, all their personal issues aside, the depths of Cole were as sexy as hell.

She was so lost in her thoughts that she didn't hear Cole's phone buzz, but the next thing she knew he was touching a hand to her shoulder. 'Jodie, someone needs our help. Let's go.'

CHAPTER EIGHT

COLE GLANCED AT Jodie's profile in the sunshine as he took the side road by the old stone chapel. She was scanning the fields from the passenger seat. Her hair was falling in wisps from her ponytail around her face, and her rosy cheeks were flushed from the cold. He'd always liked her best without make-up.

It was strange to have her with him out on call, but thankfully the tension had eased somewhat since they'd locked horns earlier. Someone had called to say they'd seen an injured stray dog wandering along an A-road.

It was almost seven-thirty a.m. The sky was a clear blue for the first time in days.

'There she is,' Jodie cried suddenly, making him hit the brakes. Ziggy started barking instantly from his demoted position in the back seat.

'I see her,' he said, pulling over quickly and making his sunglasses slide across the dashboard. Jodie caught them expertly and jumped from the car. The stray was limping awkwardly, tongue lolling out, seemingly disoriented. 'Stay here, boy,' Cole said to Ziggy before he could follow them. 'And be quiet. We don't want to scare our patient.'

Jodie was beside him on the ground in seconds. 'A husky mix, I guess,' she said as they drew closer. The creature had started to snarl. 'Look at those eyes.'

'Almost as blue as yours,' he noted out loud.

'So you think you can charm me like your horses,' she chided, though she was fighting a smile. 'She's really scared, poor thing. We need to get closer.'

The sun was streaming down now, blinding on the snow. It cast a bright spotlight on the dog's injuries as it whimpered and shivered. The blood on her left back leg was a sinister sight against the shrill morning song of the little egrets in the trees.

'Looks like she was hit by a car.' Jodie went to creep closer with him, but in seconds the creature seemed possessed, growling and snarling even more, baring its teeth. She stepped back quickly, just as Cole forged ahead. He held both hands to the ground at his sides, stayed still and quiet, asserting his dominance, making it clear he wasn't moving. 'We're not going to hurt you,' he crooned.

It was a stand-off for a good few minutes. Cole felt Jodie's eyes on him the whole time, but eventually the dog got to its belly in the snow and let out a deep sigh before starting to whimper.

'She's letting us approach her,' he said, signalling to Jodie. 'Let's get her to the car.'

Cole scooped the dog up gently in his arms and carried her to the back of the Land Rover. Jodie rushed ahead to pull the boot open, and as he laid the scruffy stray in the back he knew Jodie had noticed the same thing he just had.

'I think she's…'

'Look at her, all swollen under here,' Jodie interjected, before he could finish. 'She has puppies around here somewhere.' She pulled on gloves and rummaged for the stethoscope in his bag, then ran a check, trailing gentle hands along the dog's blood-soaked fur. 'No sounds of trauma or fluid,' she told him, visibly relieved. 'But we'll need to run some X-rays back at West Bow… I mean Everleigh.'

'Lock her in the crate while I check for the pups,' Cole told her, not missing her slip of the tongue. She had Edinburgh on the brain. He didn't suppose that would change anytime soon, but he'd realised earlier that he would have to start making her stay more enjoyable. He didn't want the bad blood between them to deny her this time at Everleigh, or a say in its future, and he didn't want Emmie to miss out either. Emmie loved Everleigh already, he could see it in her eyes—exactly the same dusky blue as Jodie's.

Sweeping snow-covered branches aside, keeping an eye out for wriggling puppies, he heard Jodie back by the vehicle, talking to the dog. She was calmer now, at least. She always was around the animals, like him. He was glad they were working together now. Their love for animals surpassed any of their personal rubbish, and he was thankful for that at least.

'Puppies! Here, pups. Where are you? We're looking for you.' He approached a ditch with a trickle of a stream running through it.

To his relief, the tiny whimper of a puppy caught his ear on the breeze and led him to a drainpipe. Crouching low in the dirt and slush, he pulled out his phone and shone the flash-light inside. Junk food wrappers tussled with the wind but behind them…

'Three puppies,' he confirmed aloud, just as Jodie reached him. Her hand landed absently on his back over his jacket as they peered inside the tiny space together. 'We have to get them out, they're still suckling.' The flashlight revealed their scruffy bodies, writhing around, trying to escape his light. 'No chance of crawling in there, though.'

'We need to lure them out with food.' Jodie's eyes narrowed, then lit up. 'I saw some biscuits in the car!'

She was back on her feet and sprinting back to the Land Rover before Cole could even feel embarrassed about the open packet of oatmeal cookies he'd left in the door.

She came back with them and he grimaced, jamming his phone back in his pocket. 'What can I say? A man gets hungry on the road.' He crumbled bits of the biscuits at the entrance to the drainpipe, annoyed he'd run out of the dog treats he usually kept in the car, and together they stood back, waiting.

'A man like you needs real food,' Jodie told him, fixing her eyes on the drainpipe entrance.

'Like your curry?' He wrinkled his nose into the middle distance, smirking.

'Hey!' She swiped at him, but again her annoyance was pretend and he dodged her, chuckling. They both knew Jodie had always been a terrible cook. She'd tried to make him a curry once. Instead of adding two teaspoons of curry powder she'd added two tablespoons.

'To be fair, you struggled through that masala most valiantly,' she said.

'I only needed about three litres of water to help.'

Jodie rolled her eyes. She'd wanted to treat him. She'd banned the staff from the kitchen and danced around in cowboy boots and cut-off denim shorts, dropping kisses on his lips between spilling rice and spices and French wine all over the place.

He still had a photo from that night, stashed away in a box. It was of both of them hunched over the bad curry, pulling faces.

He remembered another photo now. Casper had one framed of the two of them with Mustang. He'd hung it on the wall as a surprise when the cabin was finished, but Cole had taken it down again. He hadn't harboured any emotional attachment to Diyana after breaking things off with her, but the photos of Jodie had always made him miss her unbearably. He'd found a whole stash of them once—he couldn't even remember where he'd put them now.

He shoved his hands in his pockets, resisting the sudden ill-advised urge to put an arm around her. He knew she had her guard up around him, even when it looked like she was letting it down. She was well within her rights to be cautious, he supposed, but he should probably seize the opportunity to talk while she wasn't spitting fire.

'So, it seems like you're still pretty close with Ethan,' he said, testing. He was itching to ask what had gone wrong with the marriage.

Jodie just sighed. 'He's the father of my child. We still care about each other a lot. In fact, I'd say we're pretty good friends.'

He took his hands from his pockets at exactly the same time as she brushed the hem of her jacket and their fingers touched.

A flashback came into his mind. Chesil Beach. They'd been 'friends' then but he'd held her hand for the first time, and she hadn't let go for a good ten minutes. He must have been twelve, maybe thirteen. He'd been in love with her even then, but she'd had no clue. He'd hardly shown it as he'd been too caught up inside his head, figuring out how to keep her and everyone he loved away from his father's angry mouth and fists.

A squeal.

'They're coming out!' Jodie dropped to her haunches. Cole signalled for her to wait behind him while he stepped towards the pipe and scooped the tiny puppies up, one by one.

'They're so little! They don't look hurt.' Jodie stepped close, her boots next to his as she took them in her arms. For a moment their eyes met over the fuzzy bundles and they shared a smile that made him want to close the gap and kiss her, for old times' sake.

She would probably slap him if he did, he thought in vague amusement as she carried the squealing trio to the car. He swiped up a blanket from the back seat while Ziggy tried his best to reclaim the passenger seat.

'Keep them in the front with you,' he said, flinging open the passenger door for Jodie and shooing Ziggy back. 'Their mother knows they're safe with us.'

'You saved their lives,' Jodie told him breathlessly, sliding into the seat, bundling up the pups in the blanket and holding them close to her chest.

Cole leaned across from outside and pulled her seat belt across under the puppies. 'My biscuits saved their lives.'

'I'm serious, Cole. They would have died if we'd left without them. You calmed the mother down enough to let us examine her.'

'That's why I'm here,' he said.

She cocked her head. 'Because dogs need you more than elephants?'

'I guess so.' He paused, clicking the seat belt into place, stopping himself an inch from her lips again. He watched her blue eyes rake over his mouth for just a split second and wondered if she'd been thinking the same—about all the passion they'd once poured into their kisses. All the sparks and sexual tension between them had made for some pretty hot times around Everleigh once he'd finally worked up the courage to kiss her.

Time seemed to stop before he spoke. 'We

always did make a pretty good rescue team, you and I.'

Jodie pulled her eyes away. 'That was then, Cole.' Her tone was a warning to him not to dredge up the past any more, not to remind either of them how he'd ruined it. 'Things are different now.'

Three days later, Jodie was watching from the fence as Blaze was cantering the length of the manège, kicking up dust and showering the new yellow daffodils around the periphery with dirt. He bared his yellowed teeth in vain protest every time Cole cracked the training whip to make him change direction.

In the space of just a few days Blaze's wounds had healed exponentially and his temperament around Cole was drastically improved. There was still a long way to go. Whenever anyone besides Cole got too close, the stallion did not respond as well.

She was deep in thought when Aileen called.

'Jodie? How's it all going at Everleigh?'

'It's eventful,' she said, unable to take her eyes off Cole.

'We're still waiting for this meeting to be rescheduled. Hopefully it will happen by the end of the week. Is everything OK there?'

'The usual excitement,' Aileen answered. 'We're all thinking of you.'

Cole cracked the whip loudly behind Blaze. Ziggy barked in excitement and the stallion let out an anxious whinny. 'Maybe it's not as exciting here as there. What's happening?'

'Cole's in a training session with our…his… rescue,' she said, catching Cole's glance over the fence. He was wearing his stetson today. She knew he was probably wearing it ironically, for her sake. Casper had bought him one like it years ago at a horse show in Missouri and he'd worn it everywhere…even the bedroom. Once she'd worn it in the shower, behind the candles, because Cole had said her cowgirl silhouette in the low light was sexy. It took a week to dry.

She flushed at the memories and the slip of her tongue, calling Blaze *their* rescue. Already she was somewhat a partner in Blaze's recovery and treatments. Together she and Cole had given shots and medicines and soothing words to heal his burns, and she'd also been in with the clients. But then it had always been all hands on deck at Everleigh.

He'd been right when he'd said they'd always been on the same page about the rescue centre, and Everleigh in general. It was a special place, a unique place. Everyone knew it. There was so much room to grow.

But every time she looked at Cole, or he dared so much as hint at a flirtation with her, she felt an overriding need to escape in case he burned her again somehow. He was the only one with the power to do that. Just being around him and all his mysteries felt like walking the rim of an active volcano.

'Cole, huh?' Aileen sounded interested and Jodie realised with a frown that she was still looking at him, dreaming. 'The head vet and animal whisperer?'

'He doesn't like being called a whisperer, he's a behavioural therapist, but yes.'

'So, what's it like to be back there?' Aileen asked now. 'Is Emmie OK? Missing her friends yet?'

Jodie stopped two metres from the kennels. 'I wouldn't say that,' she answered slowly. 'She's made a new friend here. She gets to ride most days. She hasn't had a temper tantrum yet, actually...'

'Sounds like the country air is what you both needed,' Aileen chirped, right as Jodie heard the familiar tinkle of the doorbell in the background. 'Oh, I have to go. See you soon!'

Aileen hung up.

Jodie turned her face up to the greying sky. Why had she been letting herself get so frazzled in Edinburgh lately? Not even taking time out to ride with Emmie as much as she used to.

She hadn't had a real holiday in years. Not that this was a holiday by any stretch of the imagination, but all the tension with Cole aside she couldn't deny that the fresh country air was exactly what she'd been craving, without even realising it. Maybe it was the same for Emmie.

'Mum?' Emmie appeared to have noticed her now. She let herself into the kennel, scooping up a puppy from the clean concrete floor as it tried to escape, and a bespectacled Toby scrambled to his feet with a giant sheet of paper.

'Can we put this sign up?' he asked her. Jodie scanned the sign they'd made most creatively by taping four pieces of A4 paper together.

'Oh, it's…' she started, but she couldn't quite finish.

They'd drawn the words out in giant blue and

green letters with marker pens and stick-on gold stars. It was impressive work. But her heart was beating so fast at what they'd written that she thought she might need to sit down.

CHAPTER NINE

'EMMIE AND TOBY'S Canine Rescue Centre, huh?' Cole pulled his stetson into a deep dive against the splattering of rain. So much for the nicer weather. The air had held a soft-edged glimmer of spring, but it was threatening to turn into a downpour again now.

Jodie crossed her arms beside him. They were both observing the sign the kids had strung up with string across the kennel bars before Evie had called them in to lunch.

'Doesn't it remind you of something?' she prompted, putting a hand down to pet Ziggy's soft head.

'It's almost word for word what we wrote on our sign, isn't it?'

'Exactly. They even used the same colours! Don't you think that's strange?'

Cole looked up as a bigger raindrop landed with a plop on the rim of his hat. 'Strange,' he agreed.

It was all very strange around here lately. He never quite knew what mood he'd find Jodie in. One minute she was letting him in, the next she was closed off and cool.

Ordering Ziggy to stay outside, he let himself into the kennel and checked on their husky-cross patient. The puppies were snuggled close, suckling. 'They're doing fine, just like Mama,' he said to Jodie.

'The kids are obsessed with them. Just like we were obsessed with whatever dogs we kept in here. Remember the Westie, Deefer?'

He laughed under his breath, scooped up a puppy, checked its ears. Deefer had followed them home one summer from outside the Crow and Bell pub. Jodie had called him Dee-fer-Dog.

'Wasn't there a tabby, too? You called him called Cee-fer-Cat. I always did appreciate your unique ability for naming stray animals.'

'Emmie has more of an imagination than me.' She smiled. 'Did she tell you what she named this lot? Starchild, Archibald and Lucy-Fur. I can't even remember which one is which.'

Cole chuckled, which seemed to make Jodie laugh too, albeit behind her hair so he wouldn't see. 'She can make up all the names she wants,' he said in a flush of affection, just as a rumble of thunder pierced the sky and made the dogs' ears prick up. 'We've got more pups coming soon. We'll have a puppy overload this spring at this rate. Let's take these guys into the house before the storm hits.'

Jodie was quiet as they left the kennel with the puppies in their arms. Was she thinking how she and Emmie might not even get to see the new litter arrive, if they left Everleigh before the weekend? She seemed to be keeping her guard up around him just as much as ever but perhaps she was reluctant to discuss anything about the will, or Casper's plans for her here, until she'd spoken to Ethan. He couldn't help feeling annoyed that his name came up so often. But, then, she'd seemed just as irked by that photo of Diyana.

'It's nice, how you've taken Toby under your wing,' Jodie said, as they neared the source of the hot soup and toasted cheese sandwiches they could smell, blowing to them on the wind from the main house kitchen. 'Is that because Casper did the same for you?'

'I never really thought about it that way,' he

said, truthfully. 'Toby's dad doesn't seem to want much to do with him.'

'You didn't spend much time with your father either, did you? Before he was locked up, I mean? You were always at Everleigh. At least you were whenever I was here.'

'Maybe I just liked it more here,' he said quickly, but Jodie was studying him quizzically again.

'I was thinking before about how you never asked me to come back to your home.'

The depth of her stare made him uncomfortable.

His face must have darkened, thinking about the fists that had beaten him blue and thrown him across the living room, every time he'd gone home dirty, or late, or with an expression his father thought was rude or accusing. He'd taken it on the chin, literally, but he'd had to, or else his father would have hurt someone else instead. Like his mother, or Jodie. He couldn't imagine now, as an adult, that he would have carried out his threats, but as a child he'd had such a hold on Cole he'd been forced to take him seriously.

'And now here you are. You never left Dorset,' Jodie said, taking the wooden steps up to the main house porch. 'Apart from when you went out to Sri Lanka.'

'And college. I wouldn't have stuck it out if it hadn't been for Casper landing me the scholarship. I won't lie, that was tough, being stuck in all those soulless rooms.'

'I bet,' she said. 'Especially for someone like you.'

He nodded, grateful for the change of subject. He wasn't going to say it because who knew, it might have been the same if he'd gone to Edinburgh but he'd struggled in London, away from the horses, and Dorset. In classes all they'd seemed to do was link the minutiae of anatomy and physiology to how they might one day use it in practice. He'd found it hard to see why most of it was important at the time, all the biochemical pathways, the laws and legislations of the vet world. Casper had known better. The qualifications had taken him around the world. Cole's *other* skills had made him his fortune.

Cole nudged the farmhouse door open and put down the two puppies he was holding. Emmie ran over and picked them up instantly as Ziggy slipped inside and shook his wet coat, making her squeal.

Toby took the other pup from Jodie. 'Don't feed them anything bad,' Cole told him. 'We'll be back in a second. Gotta get these muddy boots off or we'll be in trouble.' He winked at them and closed the door again.

'Casper would have done anything for you, Cole,' Jodie continued thoughtfully. 'He knew you were an investment, too, in Everleigh's future.'

Cole murmured noncommittally and dropped to the bench outside the door. He hadn't told her his own net worth—he loathed discussing anything to do with finances. Growing up at home after the strawberry crops had failed, the topic had caused nothing but arguments between his parents. It was the reason his dad had turned to whisky. Then violence.

He was sure it would come up in the meeting with the solicitor anyway—the comfortable sums that had amounted in his bank account since people had started seeking out his skills. He'd ploughed a lot of it into wildlife rehabilitation projects and funding research projects globally, and he had still more to invest in the rescue centre when the time came, but whatever happened with the estate it was safe to say his own future was more than secure. He'd made sure of that.

'This isn't just about the money, Jodie,' he said firmly, shaking off a boot, realising she was looking at him for a reply of some kind. 'I would never sell my share of this place, you know that.'

She looked up from where she was untying her laces. 'And you still think I have no reason to either?'

'That's not what I said.'

He saw the start of an argument in her eyes, but she turned to the floor, as if thinking better of it. He took off the stetson. It was dotted with water…like the day Jodie had stepped out of the shower with it on and it had taken a week for the leather bits to dry. She probably didn't even remember that…or maybe she did. He'd seen the way she'd looked at him earlier outside with Blaze.

Jodie was quiet for a moment. 'Can I ask you a personal question?'

'I feel like you're going to anyway.'

'Why didn't Diyana come back here with you from Sri Lanka?'

'She didn't come back here with me because I didn't ask her to.' He scraped the mud roughly from his boots across the wiry mats beneath the bench. Jodie said nothing, but he could feel the way she'd tensed up beside him.

'You're jealous,' he asserted.

'Don't be absurd. I'm not jealous, Cole.' Her voice was hoity-toity and he arched an eyebrow at her in amusement. She huffed and dropped to the seat beside him. 'OK, you win. Maybe I felt a little spark of jealousy just then...'

'Just a little one?'

'Considering our history, and the way you left things, I thought you'd be happy here with your horses, but you look so happy in that photo with her.' She paused, looked into the rain. 'The one in your kitchen with your elephant.'

'You looked pretty happy in your wedding photos, too,' he countered. 'And we'd only just broken up.'

Jodie closed her eyes. 'You didn't want me, Cole. You made that very clear.'

He couldn't stop himself now. 'You got pregnant, Jodie, *six months* after we ended things.'

'After *you* ended things, you mean.' Her voice was level, measured, but he could sense her simmering. Something made him push her.

'You slept with another guy. And then you married him.'

She stood and faced him. 'Was I supposed to call you up and ask for permission? What is this about, Cole? You told me you didn't love me, so why did you care?'

'No, I didn't. I never said I didn't love you.'

'Not in so many words but…' She paused, like she was only just considering she might have heard things he hadn't said as well as things he had. 'Anyway,' she huffed, 'both Ethan and I were totally drunk the night the accident happened…'

'Accident?' Cole gripped the bench hard beneath him as he processed this new information. 'Your pregnancy was an accident?'

'Of course it was, Cole,' she snapped. 'I was nineteen.'

She sat back down again heavily with a sigh. Thunder rumbled in the distance. 'Ethan was my good friend, my flatmate. He took the place in the flat share that *you* were supposed to take, actually. My parents wanted me to abort the baby, obviously, you know what they're like. But I couldn't do it.'

'So you *married* him?'

'Yes, but…it was more complicated than that.'

'What do you mean?'

She huffed. 'I don't want to talk about this with you.'

Cole sucked in a breath and let it out into the mounting storm. He felt his shoulders tense as her fingers started drumming on the bench beside him. So she *hadn't* loved the guy? She'd married a man she hadn't loved? Why?

He turned on the bench, took her face in his hands and brought his forehead to hers. Heat surged through him and made him hold her tighter. 'Jodie. It's *me* asking you this. Why did you marry Ethan if he was only a friend…if you'd just made a mistake? You were nineteen years old, you had everything ahead of you.'

'I told you before, we made it work.'

Her eyes had clouded over. She raised her hands over his, then back to his open jacket. Maybe they had made it work somehow. She had graduated after all, but if Cole had gone to her sooner, instead of appeasing his useless, abusive father or listening to Casper advocating caution once his father had died, she might not have married Ethan. She might have married *him*...

The smell of cheese toasties was so damn good but suddenly he'd lost his appetite. She was breathing hot and sharp against him, her fingers fisting and unfisting on his jacket. 'Jodie?'

She seemed to wrestle with her emotions and he could almost feel her walls crumbling down before she pulled away from him and composed herself. Emmie was still giggling at something in the kitchen.

'I'm not going to do this with you, Cole,' she hissed in a whisper, breaking free and making for the farmhouse door. 'How can you ask me to explain my life's decisions after you broke us and then did *nothing* to fix it? This is getting us nowhere.'

'So I set up the new account. Dacey had to approve it because technically we're too young to have social media...but you're on—see?' Emmie passed the iPad to Cole over the kitchen island and Jodie watched his eyes widen over his bowl of tomato soup.

'I've posted four photos so far,' Emmie said. 'One of the kennel with our new sign, and one of each puppy. Lucy-Fur has the most likes, so we'll use the same hashtags again for the next post. It's really trial and error, you know? We have to figure out which hashtags are more popular with people looking for rescue animals.'

'Either way,' Toby added, 'we think we'll have homes for them all by the end of next week.'

'All three puppies? Without anyone coming to see them?' Cole looked impressed, and maybe a little awed; it wasn't a look Jodie was used to seeing on Cole Crawford's face. She realised his toastie was untouched. She could tell his mind was elsewhere, churning over the information she'd just shared about Ethan, no doubt, but he was doing his best to seem normal.

'People can still come and see them.' Toby put one of the puppies down on the counter top and let it sniff around their plates. 'This just helps us weed out the most suitable owners, so we can send them a personal invite.'

'I see.' Cole took a tiny spoonful of soup and moved his bowl away from the puppy's snuffling nose.

Jodie was grateful for the kids easing the tension after what had happened outside. She wanted to blame it on the storm but she knew better—there was so much about their past together that neither of them had been expecting to still rattle them, and the explosions were getting to be a regular thing.

If he hadn't teased her about her jealousy over Diyana, she might not have been as flustered as to admit that she and Ethan had conceived Emmie by accident. She already regretted letting that slip.

OK, so she hadn't told him anything about how she and Ethan had basically been *forced* to marry or risk having to drop out of their degrees. And there was no way in hell she was admitting she'd been so weak at the time, so lost without Cole that she'd waded through most of that year not caring at all what went on around her, but, still, Cole had no business pushing her for details when he'd been the one to break things off in the first place. And he was still keeping secrets from her. She knew it.

I never said I didn't love you. She couldn't forget the way he'd just said that.

Emmie squealed with laughter as the puppy

wagged its tail against her glass of juice and sent it sliding along the counter so fast that Cole had to grab it before it toppled over the edge. Jodie went for it at the same time and her fingers landed over his.

'Be careful,' they said at the same time, catching eyes, just as a lightning bolt lit the room from outside.

Toby clapped his hands. 'I love storms.'

'You can feel the energy in the air,' Emmie said, looking between her and Cole. Jodie pulled her hand away as though she'd been stung.

Cole scooped up the puppy in one swoop and deposited it back on the floor before Evie could see and reprimand them. The bustling housekeeper was busy adding more coals to the hearth in the corner, which was already blazing with a fire.

'So, have you guys been studying marketing up in your rooms when most kids are watching cartoons?' Cole teased, stepping over the skittish puppy and crossing with his bowl to the wide copper sink.

'I never watch cartoons,' Emmie said. She was twirling her ponytail around her fingers at the back of her baseball hat. 'And it's not really marketing, Cole, it's just using common sense.'

'It's all about common sense,' Toby reiterated.

Jodie couldn't help smirking a little at the way they were putting him in his place when it came to modern technology. Emmie was pretty good at reaching her father on social media already. She'd been given a phone on her eleventh birthday for that purpose alone, but she'd never seen her daughter try to put her skills to use in this way before.

Cole was watching her now from over by the sink, drying his bowl diligently with a dishcloth. His leather jacket was undone, his jeans were smudged up one side with mud from the manège. His stetson was almost skimming a copper cooking pan that hung from the beams. She realised she'd barely touched her lunch either.

'Don't you want that soup, Mum?' Emmie asked.

'I might have some later instead,' she said, flustered. Cole was still staring at her.

'So, Cole, it looks like you've found yourself some new social media managers,' Evie said now. Had she picked up on the stormy atmosphere between them? 'Did Casper not have any social media set up for this place at all?'

'None,' Emmie answered for him, pattering over to the sink in thick pink woollen socks, with both of their bowls. 'But don't worry, Cole, Toby and I can handle it for you guys. I'm sure you and Mum have better things to do together.'

Emmie ran the hot tap, then started pulling on a pair of rubber gloves. Jodie watched in amazement. Emmie never volunteered to do her own washing-up at home, gloves or no gloves. She never even unloaded the dishwasher unless she was asked to.

She was so taken aback that it took a moment for Emmie's words and tone to sink in. Had she really just said, *I'm sure you have better things to do together?*

'We'll find the next litter of puppies homes, too. Then we can move on to any horses you bring in. There will be more after Blaze, right? Can we ride him soon? Oh, can we go to Green Vale with Dacey and Vinny tomorrow for the animal show?'

Emmie was looking expectantly at Cole now.

Cole hung the dishcloth on its hook on the wall and flicked the rim of her hat affectionately with a thumb. 'So many questions,' he said. 'You're just like your mother.'

'I tend to stop, when I don't get any answers,' Jodie shot back. She regretted it when Emmie raised an eyebrow at her, then Evie. 'What's Green Vale?'

'It's my school,' Toby replied.

'I guess you could call it alternative.' Cole shrugged. 'They have some pretty interesting activities during half-term too. I'm a big fan of the woodland yoga classes.'

Jodie scoffed. She knew he was joking. At least, she *thought* he was.

'Uncle Cole helped me get a place at the new school, Ms Everleigh,' Toby explained. 'This one's way better, we have maths and geography lessons in 3D! There's no headteacher and no hierarchy, the school is jointly managed by students and staff. And we have pigs and donkeys, and we make organic lunches. Before half-term we had to learn to build a fence to keep the pigs off the vegetable patch.'

'They have a yoga studio *and* a photography lab,' Emmie added. She had clearly been told all about it already.

'And they teach them useful stuff, like debating and cooking,' Cole said. 'Not that you couldn't have learned all that at Everleigh too, right, Toby?'

Toby pulled a face. 'Maybe not cooking, not from you, Cole.'

Cole nodded sagely. 'That's fair.' Jodie stifled a snigger.

The wooden door to the practice creaked open and Dacey, one of the vets, walked in, followed by a tiny, wobbly white lamb.

Emmie and Toby both sprang from the sink and started fussing over it. 'Want to help with feeding?' Dacey said, holding up a baby bottle filled with milk. 'She was brought in this morning for a check-up after her mother died, poor sweet thing. What should we call her?'

'We'll call her Annie,' Emmie announced, before anyone else could make a suggestion. 'Like the orphan. Toby, get the iPad, can you, and take a photo of me and Annie for the new social media account. Should I wear these rubber gloves in it?'

'Yeah, that would be funny!'

All of a sudden there was a ruckus of paws and giggles and soap suds and hooves across the floor tiles, a spilled bottle of milk, the clicking iPad camera, the lamb bleating, dogs barking and rain lashing at the windows.

There was never a quiet or dull moment in the Everleigh kitchen, Jodie mused nostalgically. There had always been so many people, so many opinions flying around, so much to do. She was deeply touched that Cole cared enough about Toby to help get him into a new school, too.

They needed to talk more, clear the air. It was ridiculous, carrying all this ancient resentment and tension around—she was here for Everleigh, not Cole. They had to put all that behind them and move forward, for Emmie's sake more than hers. Emmie would only get caught in the middle if this bitterness continued.

Then…the door to the porch swung open again. The stablehand Russell stumbled in, along with a gust of wind and rain. 'C-Cole,' he stuttered, clutching his leg and wincing in pain. 'Cole, man, we have a problem.'

Evie sprang for the old-fashioned telephone on the wall. 'I'll call an ambulance.'

Dacey and Emmie both grappled to stop the lamb from fleeing out the door as Cole hurried to Russell's side. The bottom of the poor guy's jeans was soaked in mud, rain and blood.

'Blaze is gone,' Russell said, grimacing at the sight of his own leg. 'He freaked out at the lightning. I couldn't stop him.'

CHAPTER TEN

'WHY CAN'T YOU take the Land Rover? It's pouring with rain!' Jodie's blue eyes were imploring as Cole heaved the saddle over the back of one of their thoroughbred hotblood mares, Aphrodite.

'Ziggy needs to follow Blaze's scent,' he explained, yanking the straps tight on the left stirrup.

'Blaze won't have gone far *because* of the rain,' he told her. 'But he doesn't know the area so he could be anywhere.'

'I'll come with you.' Jodie was hot on their heels. She was already wearing a riding helmet she'd plucked from the wall and wielding a bridle, awaiting instructions. 'Which horse can I take?'

'You're not coming with me, Jodie,' he told her, hurrying down the aisle with Aphrodite. 'It's too dangerous. I need you alive.'

'Don't be ridiculous.'

He knew she was concerned for his safety, but he was more concerned for hers. Cole was kicking himself for not checking in when the storm started. He'd been distracted by Jodie, and the cozy mayhem in the kitchen. What had happened to Russell was *his* fault.

At the door he prepared to mount, but Jodie's willowy frame blocked him.

'Tell me which horse or I'll take Mustang.'

'Mustang couldn't keep up.'

'Then give me another one. Stop trying to protect me, you're acting like I've never ridden before when you know damn well I'm as capable as you are. What if you need my help when you find him?'

'Fine.' She wouldn't back down, he knew it. Admittedly he was treating her unfairly. 'If you insist. Grab the saddle.' He took the bridle from her and clasped his hands around her waist. He heard her gasp as he put a hand to her pert backside and hoisted her onto Aphrodite's back with one swift movement.

'Do your helmet up,' he ordered as she landed astride the horse. He threw her up the reins. 'I'll saddle up Pirate.'

They took to the road and Ziggy set off ahead, nose to the ground around the rain-crushed daffodils.

Blaze had kicked Russell in the shins, charged past him on the way out of the manège and leapt over the gate to the property like it was nothing but an oxer in a lower showjumping division. A wounded, frightened stallion like him on the loose yet again was a serious liability.

'Has Ziggy done this before?' Jodie called out from behind him.

'He can find anything,' he shouted back against the wind.

They'd only been out on short, fun rides with Emmie and Toby so far, but this was something different. Secretly he thrived on the adrenaline, especially with Jodie at his side…but she was a mother now. Things were not the same as they had been before, so he had even *more* reasons to be careful with her.

Near The Ship Inn, Ziggy suddenly let out three sharp barks at the crossroads by the old red phone box.

'He's got something!' Jodie yelled.

'Get closer to me,' he called to her. He trusted

the mare in all weather conditions, but he needed to be able to grab Jodie's reins if anything *did* go wrong.

The mud and dirt splattered Aphrodite's pristine grey legs as they broke into a gallop. Ziggy led them down side roads, across a field of cows. Jodie's helmet did nothing to stop the rain drenching the ends of her hair.

Cole ran over their previous conversation as his horse pounded a new gravel track beneath him and the cold wind whipped his face. He was surprised he'd managed to hold a conversation with the kids at lunch, knowing that Jodie had probably only got married to save face after getting pregnant. She hadn't admitted it, she was likely too embarrassed, but why else would she have married a friend?

Shifting his weight to his outside hip, he nudged his heel into Pirate's right side, and Pirate picked up the pace in perfect rhythm. He could almost see Casper on the horizon, as he always had been before, riding up ahead of him.

This had been their place, where they'd made all their troubles disappear. Just listening to the steady pounding of hooves, the tail-swishes, it had always put his mind at ease, but so had their conversations. Except one, he thought now, back when Casper had told him Jodie was pregnant and getting married. He thought back to writing the letter that same night. He hadn't thought about it in a long time. He had told Jodie everything in that letter. Would it have made a difference for *them* if he'd sent it?

He considered giving it to her now.

No, he couldn't. If she found out this late how he'd broken it off to try and save her like some storybook hero… God, she would never forgive him. She might not regret having the amazing Emmie, but he'd sent her off into some other guy's arms, who'd got her pregnant by *mistake*. All that, just because he'd never had the guts to face up to his father and call his bluff.

'Do you see anything yet?' Jodie was breathless and flushed and her jeans were drenched as she came up alongside him on her horse.

'Nothing, but I trust that dog.'

Some way up the path, Ziggy upped his barking, urging them down an even narrower path at the side of some old storage barns. 'The river's down there,' he yelled to Jodie. 'It runs through the woods. Follow me, it could be dangerous in this wind.'

Cole had been bucked off, bitten, kicked and bowled over himself over the years…but he'd also never, ever blamed a horse for its hostility. Horses were aggressive for two reasons only: if they felt threatened, or if they'd been taught to dominate humans. There was every chance Blaze would feel threatened if they cornered him in the woodland. He'd have to take the chance.

'Go slowly, please,' Jodie urged him, close behind him on the narrow trail. 'You don't know what he's capable of.'

'I won't let anything happen to you,' he told her. He would protect her at all costs. Maybe it was in his biological make-up, or maybe it came from sheltering her for all those years. Maybe it would always be in his wiring, he didn't know, but he felt it like a duty. To this day, he would put Jodie's safety and well-being over his own, in any situation.

The storm seemed to be subsiding, and the rain was finally easing off. Jodie remembered the gushing river to her left. Casper had warned them about the fierce undercurrents when they were kids, especially after heavy rain. It was bulging now, after all the snowmelt they'd had.

Casper's words came to Jodie's mind as Cole crouched down in the sodden moss and leaves, two metres from an anxious-looking Blaze. *'The most dangerous part of a horse is its feet, Jodie.'*

In a heartbeat, Blaze bucked beneath a giant oak, sending the birds scattering. With a gut-wrenching whinny he charged at Cole, kicking up the leaves in a power play.

'Jodie, don't move an inch,' Cole warned. He didn't even make a move himself, but the horse swerved at the last second and made for the rushing river.

'There's nowhere to go, bud,' she heard him say calmly. He inched towards him again, swiping at low-hanging branches.

Blaze trotted manically up and down what exposed bit of riverbank he could get a footing on. The stallion's neck was lathered in a thick sweat, more from his nerves than from the warmth of the sun, she could tell. His wounds and scars, lit up in a shaft of sudden sunlight, were almost unbearable to see.

The meds had brought him a long way, and his ribs weren't as prominent. But she knew the scars on the inside must be painful for him to act like this, especially when Cole had already worked so hard on gaining his trust.

'Cole, please be careful,' she heard herself say. He wasn't even wearing a hard hat. She almost threw him hers but he put a hand up to stop her, to keep her still.

She was sweating now as she stood there, clutching their horses' reins. One kick from Blaze to Cole's head, and his face would look worse than Russell's shin, if he even survived at all, but she trusted he knew what he was doing.

Blaze was eyeing Cole suspiciously, creating showers of wet chestnut leaves, mud and torn-up daffodils. His scorched nose snorted air. His ears were pinned back and his head jerked this way and that as Cole crept ever closer to the riverbank.

Jodie felt like she'd gone at least ten minutes without taking a breath. But thankfully it wasn't long before Blaze's ears returned to normal, and she watched in wonder as the horse lowered his head in apparent surrender.

'Good man, you know you can trust us.' Cole

got close enough to fix the bridle over Blaze's head. Jodie drew a sigh of relief when she saw the reins in his hands. Finally, he was back in control.

She turned to mount Aphrodite…but a sudden commotion behind her made her spin back.

Cole yelled something to her about a rabbit, right before Blaze reared up in fright. The next part seemed to happen in slow motion. Before she could get a mental grip on the situation, Cole was forced backwards into the river.

'Cole!' Jodie raced to the edge and made a futile grab for his billowing shirt. The river was freezing. To her horror, in a nanosecond she couldn't see him at all.

She tore off her jacket, ready to jump in and swim after him…where to, she had no idea. Ziggy was barking hysterically. She saw the dog crouch before she could stop him. 'Ziggy, no!'

With a giant leap Ziggy dived in and started paddling furiously. She flailed for his tail but he drifted out of reach. The world went white and then back to colour.

She couldn't see Cole, still. Maybe he'd hit his head. The thought filled her with sheer terror. A thousand possible scenarios made her feel sick to her stomach as she scanned the river surface up ahead. *Where was Cole?*

A thud in her side almost knocked her fully into the water. Blaze's reins. Grabbing them in one fist, she held on so tight that her hands blistered instantly beneath the leather. With her other hand, she fisted tufts of grass to steady herself, and realised what the horse was doing.

Blaze was trotting in a strange dance, backwards from the riverbank, stomping over shrubs and flowers, biting and yanking on the reins, which were attached to…

Cole. Cole still had hold of the reins.

'Jodie! Don't move. It's OK.' She heard his voice before she saw him. Thank God, he was conscious.

He was getting closer to her now, bobbing back towards her on the white lip of the current. He almost collided with Ziggy but somehow he scooped the struggling dog up in one arm and held him protectively.

Blaze was pulling him back in. Jodie couldn't believe what she was seeing. Foam was still frothing at the corners of the horse's mouth from the sheer effort, but the whole thing had happened in seconds, maybe thirty at the most.

Blaze had purposely lengthened the line between them and was using his strength to pull Cole back in from the water. He was saving Cole's life.

CHAPTER ELEVEN

'PARACETAMOL… ASPIRIN… I need something.' Her nerves were shot. 'Cole, where do you keep your medicine?' She knew he couldn't hear her as he was in the shower.

She pulled open the middle drawer, the top drawer, the bottom drawer… Nothing but cutlery, pens, cables, dog treats. He hadn't told her where it was. He'd insisted he was fine, but she knew he'd be in pain soon enough, if he wasn't already.

They'd ridden the horses back slowly, with Blaze beside them. Cole was bleeding under his jacket, she'd seen it when she'd peeled it off him as soon as they'd reached the cabin, but he'd brushed off his injury. 'Go shower, get warm,' he 'd told her.

So she had, and now she was back. How could she leave him? Russell was in the hospital, and she could tell Cole blamed himself

for not checking on Blaze sooner. She knew
the way his brain was wired. He would never
blame a horse.

*You could have lost him. He could have
drowned.*

The thought was like a knife wound to her
heaving chest as tears threatened to consume
her.

'Where would you keep your medicine?' she
said to his kitchen walls, moving mugs and coffee flasks, and an empty bread bin. Cole would
keep the medicine somewhere odd, she thought,
like under the sofa.

Her eyes caught on something under the
bench by the door, covered in jackets.

Dropping to her knees in her track pants,
she pulled out the bright red medicine kit and
flipped the latch under the huge white cross.
Paracetamol. That would have to do.

She slid the box back, but it was stuck now,
jammed halfway out. Reaching behind, it her
hands landed on something smooth, made of
glass. She pulled out a photo frame covered in
dust and swept a hand across it.

Cole and her, sitting on Mustang, bareback.

She fell on her bottom, holding it.

There was another box, she noticed now—the box his stetson had arrived in. She slid it out from under the bench and sifted through photos from their summers together. *He'd kept all these?*

One fell out.

There was Cole, looking up at her from the floor, leaning with his arms crossed and his leg kicked back against a red tractor. She was behind him in the photo, grinning from the driver's seat. It must have been taken the first summer they'd met.

There was Casper in another one, just as she remembered him in his trademark waxed cotton cap and quilted moleskin jacket, with one arm around her shoulders and the other holding a chicken.

Another photo. Her and Cole at twelve or thirteen. She recognised Chesil Beach—this must have been the day they'd gone on a fossil hunt. She held it closer, studying his tanned hand wrapped tightly around hers on their bucket of treasures. That had been around the time that parts of her had started tingling in anticipation of his touch. Just his hand, hauling her up to a rock for a photo, had felt like another moment in heaven.

Another photo. Her and Cole at fourteen. Cole was even more tanned in this one, holding a pitchfork like a guitar out in the stables. He'd been skinny before but now he was filling out. He had muscles from labouring with hay bales and farming equipment, and a wild mop of curls. This was right before he'd taught her to ride bareback, solo, she remembered with a smile.

This was the summer she'd thought Cole was finally going to kiss her...but he didn't. The kiss had come at fifteen. There was no photo from that year, but she could see it as clear as day. They'd been swimming in the river, looking for kingfishers. Cole had swum right up to her beneath the wrought-iron bridge.

She'd thought he'd been about to dunk her; she'd been laughing and splashing him in his new blue board shorts. She'd been self-conscious of her new womanly body, and awed by his new broad chest and the thick, dark hair in places he hadn't had hair before. But his hands had found her waist under the water. Without a word, he had pulled her into the shadows under the bridge and kissed her. Her first kiss. Cole had been her first everything.

Jodie pressed her bare feet to the cold tile floor, clutching the photos to her heart as the mental image of Cole slipping away in the river tore a new hole in her chest. They'd had their disagreements and spent the last twelve years apart but if anything happened to him she knew she would die herself, even after all this time.

The tears wouldn't stop now. She didn't know how long she sat there, falling apart, on the floor, but Ziggy laid a sympathetic head on her lap and she was very grateful for the comfort.

A sound from the bathroom made Jodie shove the photos and medicine kit back, but a letter slipped out from the pile. At least it looked like a letter, sealed in a cream-coloured envelope. There was nothing on the front, but she recognised the old-fashioned wax stamp Casper had always used, sealing the back closed.

Hearing Cole moving about, she put it back with the photos and laid the framed photo back on top, wiping her dusty hand on her tracksuit bottoms.

By the time Cole stepped from the bathroom, running a towel over his hair, in nothing but clean jeans, she was stoking the fire, trying to dry her eyes, as well as her wet hair and damp tank top.

'How are you feeling?' he asked her, dropping to the leather couch then wincing at the pain to his shoulder.

'Better than you, I think,' she said, still fighting to gain control of her shaky voice and limbs. He was here, he was OK, and she had to pull herself together.

The buckle of his jeans blazed red from the fire behind her. Her eyes fell to the lines on his body from his belt to the trail of dark fuzz up to his belly button. Shuffling between his knees on the rug, she popped the paracetamol from their foil case.

It had been a long time since she'd seen Cole without his shirt on. He looked even better now than he had then, only he was still bleeding.

'You're really hurt, Cole.'

'I told you, I'm fine.'

'That's what you always say, Cole, even when you're not.'

He tipped up her chin with a finger, looking her deep in the eyes. 'Hey, I'm sorry I scared you.'

'What if you'd died, the same way your dad did?'

Cole's face darkened. 'I'd have hoped more people would miss me.'

The shadows on his abs caused a flicker of a memory. One hot second of them making love. Then another memory, years before they'd been an item, of Cole telling her he'd broken his finger. It had been over Christmas, when she'd been back in Greenwich, so they'd talked about it on the phone.

When she'd offered to fly down on Christmas Day to be with him, he'd told her not to be so dramatic. *'I told you Jodie, I'm fine. It was an accident, he didn't mean to...'*

'Who didn't mean to?'

'The dog, when it jumped up at the door and slammed it shut on me! Tell me what's going on with you?'

She took his strong, gentle hand on his lap, opened his palm and put the pills in it. Why was she remembering that now? Because he was in pain and embarrassed that someone might want to help him?

'Swallow,' she said, reaching a tentative finger to his wound. His right upper arm was bruised from a collision with a rock.

'You got lucky, you won't need stitches,' she told him, but his skin was already a wicked shade of purple around the cuts. His biceps stretched out another deep red scratch as he chased the pills with water from a mug.

'Cole, that horse saved your life today.'

His gaze fell to her lips, right before he leaned across her to put the mug down, sending the scent of familiar musky soap to her nose, deep to her core. 'Not many people would believe that.' Her stomach flipped as he caught her fingers and pressed a hard kiss to her knuckles.

'I saw what he did. I saw Ziggy dive in after you, too,' she managed, though her heart was thrumming.

He cradled her face in his hand, and his thumb caressed her cheek. She leaned into him, closing her eyes. Every nerve ending flared at his touch.

'I need to tell you something,' he said.

She held her breath. Her gut told her she wasn't going to like this.

'Casper left a photo of you out on his desk, not long after he got back from your wedding in Edinburgh.' Cole ran a finger softly across her lower lip, sending a flock of butterflies straight between her legs. 'Seeing you in that white dress, married to someone else, knowing you were carrying his baby... Do you want to know what I did?'

'What?'

'I rode Mustang out to West Bay cliffs. I yelled at the sea until my throat was on fire, and you know I never yell. A guy with a dog ran over and asked if I was OK.'

'Jealousy almost drove you off a cliff, huh?' Jodie joked weakly, swiping her hair behind her ear. 'And yet you never once tried to come and get me back.'

The rug was hot under her knees as she knelt between his legs. He lowered his head, urging her lips ever closer. Her fingers inched around the waist of his jeans, tracing across his hip bone before curling about his belt, urging him down from the couch to the floor without any words. He let out an anguished groan as he slid to the rug, still lacing his fingers through her hair, keeping her head close enough to kiss.

'Why didn't you try to get me back, Cole?'

'All this time, I thought you'd fallen in love with someone else.'

They seemed to hover there in silent longing, until she'd had enough. She crushed her lips to his. She wanted…no, needed him. All of him. Cole's body loosened. His arms encircled her like a cage, more possessive by the moment.

'You have no idea how much I missed you,' he growled against her lips, as his fingers found her bra straps and slid them down her shoulders.

She realised he probably meant he'd missed their amazing sex but she wasn't about to ruin the moment with more questions.

In seconds he was worshipping her bare breasts with his lips and kisses in the firelight, and her breathing was ragged and raspy in his hair. He urged her down onto the sheepskin rug, hovering over her, taking her in. She was older now than when they'd last been together like this, and she wasn't used to a man's gaze on her body, not the way Cole was looking at her.

His eyes showed nothing but admiration and

lust as she traced her fingers along the lines of his abs. He knelt between her legs, reached up and pulled his shirt over his head, tossing it to the couch. He was all man; broader, bigger, muscled from a life outdoors intensified by lifting saddles and straw bales and labouring over the gardens at Everleigh.

Every muscle on his torso rippled in the firelight. Their bickering and unresolved issues seemed to melt away. She blocked it all out, or rather her tendons, muscles and limbs ignored her head and its burning questions. The thrill of his touch was too intense to deny.

Heat was all she felt. Heat from the fire, heat from Cole, heat from the sparks between them as he came back over her, his good arm getting lost in the sheepskin rug as he trailed a finger from his other hand over her breasts, slowly down to her belly, tracing more delicious kisses in its wake. His close-trimmed beard left trails of delicious tingles on her skin.

She'd used to love it when he'd worshipped her like this, sometimes more than the act of making love itself. The gentle, teasing touch, as soft as a moth on her skin, created tingles of anticipation all over her.

Lying on her back, Jodie shivered at his touch, arching from the rug to allow him to lower her sweatpants, then allowing a pent-up moan to escape her throat as his fingers found the once-familiar path to the parts of her that only *he* had ever known how to truly make tremble.

'I'll stop if you want me to.'

Somewhere in a distant galaxy another version of herself screamed *Yes, stop*, but in his hands she was mute, relishing in the chemistry bubbling and fizzing between them. It was theirs and theirs alone.

His fingers wove through hers on the rug above her head, and every few kisses he squeezed them tight, as if he needed to check if she was really there with him, doing this, after all this time. She was here, she realised, heart and soul, inching out of her underwear with her lips still glued to his.

'Jodie…' He stopped, as if to question their actions again, or tell her something he'd been keeping to himself. She couldn't tell, but she didn't care now. She was already gone, into him, consumed by him. Her naked body seemed to remember his, like a song that had been on the tip of her tongue but which she'd somehow forgotten the words to till now. They didn't need words, she remembered that now. Making love had always been their principal means of communication.

'How is your daughter doing?' Jodie asked the solicitor, crossing her legs under the desk in fitted green military-style trousers that she knew Cole hadn't seen before. She'd felt his eyes on her bottom walking in here, but she hadn't known quite how to look him in the eyes yet.

Ms Tanner looked up from the papers on the desk between them. 'It was nothing serious but she's much better now. Thank you for asking. Again, I'm sorry this meeting had to be rescheduled. My husband was away on business so there was no one else to watch her.'

'It's not a problem. It gave us time to...' Cole trailed off, catching Jodie's eye as Ziggy stretched out across his feet under the desk. Her insides jolted. She could still feel the slight burn of his kisses on her lips and an echo of euphoria that was now disguising itself as mild discomfort between her legs—the kind of physical afterglow you only ever experienced after making love more times than you can remember in one night.

It didn't take much to send her mind back to how she'd melted into him, but in the cold light of day she was starting to regret her raging libido already. *Time to what?* She wondered what he'd been about to say. Time to fall back into bed together? Of course he wouldn't say that in front of the solicitor, but what if he was thinking it?

She'd given herself to him willingly, and she wasn't particularly proud of that. Whatever force of gravity that had seemed to bring her body back to his had left her reeling and fumbling through the morning, wondering what the hell had happened to her brain.

They'd both returned to earth to find missed calls from Ms Tanner about the meeting. Jodie had almost forgotten they still had to talk with her.

'You were lucky. Casper had this all planned out,' the round-faced, flame-haired Irishwoman told them from the leather-backed chair.

'For how long?'

Ms Tanner leafed through the pages in front

of her with neatly manicured fingers. 'For almost five years.'

'Five years?' Jodie was stunned. Cole dragged a hand through his hair. She knew he was probably still in pain from yesterday. He hadn't exactly been careful with his arm, rolling around in the living room with her all night, but he was doing his best to hide any discomfort.

'We find it's better to initiate conversations about estates by focusing on the owner's wishes and concerns, rather than on who gets what,' Ms Tanner explained, pushing her glasses up her nose. 'So that's what we focused on when Casper came to us. The potential long-term care needs he had in mind for Everleigh came back to you, Mr Crawford, and you, Ms Everleigh.'

'Ms Tanner, can I see that plan?'

'Of course.' She slid the papers over the desk to Jodie. 'You're free to look over all this again in your own time. You can come to an agreement between yourselves. If selling is on your mind at the end of the stipulated time spent here, Ms Everleigh, you should know there are legal arrangements already in place regarding which assets are held for designated beneficiaries without the need for a court process...'

Jodie scanned the documents, listening dutifully, swigging from her coffee cup as Ziggy warmed her cold feet as well as Cole's, like the dog had accepted her into his pack already.

She hadn't even contemplated probate, or the prospect of divvying up what would be hers and what would be Cole's. That would feel more like a separation than the day he'd broken up with her; not that splitting away from Cole in any way, shape or form should bother her now, she thought defiantly.

And yet here we are now...

They'd just made incredible love and her heart was rioting in her chest.

'Do you have any thoughts about selling, Mr Crawford?' Ms Tanner asked him.

Cole sat up straighter on his chair. Again Jodie noticed him trying not to wince at his shoulder pain—stubborn fool. 'This is my home,' he stated bluntly. 'I'm not going anywhere, and I wouldn't particularly want anyone else coming in as a partner either. Jodie knows what Casper wanted for this place better than anyone.'

She caught his eyes again and he held them this time, searching hers like he was waiting for her to either agree, or thank him, or maybe even confirm here and now that she wouldn't be selling anything either, once she'd done what Casper had asked of her.

Shame, guilt and irritation flared up out of nowhere. She'd put herself in an awkward situation last night. She'd been so caught up in Cole and the moment that she'd completely forgotten she was supposed to be staying away from the man who'd, oh, so casually ripped the rug out from under her once. She might know Everleigh better than anyone else who might walk in off the street, wanting a piece of it, but she owed Cole nothing. He was the one who'd kept her away from here for so long in the first place by ending their relationship.

And yet you still slept with him!

She tried to squish the delicious flashback of their bodies moving as one, the absence of space and time, or past and future that she'd felt in his arms. She owed him nothing. She'd just been weakened in the moment, seeing all those photos, remembering how she'd loved him once.

But it had felt so incredible. Like nothing else mattered.

Cole was still looking at her, and Ms Tanner

cleared her throat, as though sensing the tension. 'Well, from your personal financial statements I see you're quite comfortable here, in more ways than one, Mr Crawford. And as for you, Ms Everleigh, I see you fare the same in Scotland. You are of course entitled to review the situation once the conditions stated in the will have been met in a year's time.'

'I'm aware of that, thank you,' Jodie said. 'As you can imagine, it's quite a lot of information to take in. I owe it to my ex-husband, Ethan, to discuss this with him. Neither of us would want our daughter or her education to be disrupted. I also have my own practice and staff to consider in Edinburgh, so I can imagine selling my share of Everleigh at the end of the year is probably still quite likely.'

'I quite understand. Maybe you'll feel differently in a year.'

Jodie chewed her cheek. Beside her, Cole's jaw had started to spasm. Ziggy seemed to sense the general air of discomfort and whimpered softly as Jodie shook her head. What was she supposed to do?

Reality was probably taking a fist to Cole's ego right now and her suspicions were getting the better of her. If he thought one night of sex…even if it was the best sex they'd ever indulged in, as far as she could remember…would somehow secure her decision to keep her half of the estate, he was wrong.

Emmie was her priority now. Even if Jodie had very much enjoyed last night, *everything* she'd known for the last twelve years was in Edinburgh.

'Who's to say someone else wouldn't do a better job than me?' she added now, trying to make herself believe it at the same time. 'Someone with more time and fewer…commitments.'

'Sounds like you need this time to figure things out between yourselves,' Ms Tanner said, looking from one to the other.

'Or to find another suitable partner for Cole,' Jodie added.

Cole had a face like thunder now but he remained silent and stony. Ms Tanner raised an eyebrow. Jodie swore she saw her smirk.

When the solicitor had wished them both goodbye and good luck, Jodie realised she was quite wound up. They were business partners with a sizeable fortune and even more sizeable responsibilities. Everything about the meeting had hammered that home.

What had she done, giving in to him like that last night? Worse than that, hadn't she initiated it?

She braced herself to take Cole aside and ensure he knew that last night had been a mistake, and that they should leave things on a platonic note and remember their priority was Everleigh going forward.

He didn't give her a chance. 'I have an appointment,' he told her curtly and strode in the direction of the stables without looking back. She watched him go, stunned.

CHAPTER TWELVE

TOBY LOOKED GENUINELY sad as he helped to put Emmie's bags in the back of their car. Emmie looked torn as she hugged one of the puppies to her for the last time. 'I can't believe you're leaving before the next puppies arrive. And we've got that girl coming to see Lucy-Fur later.'

'I have to get back to school, and Saxon.'

'But you'll be back soon, right?'

Emmie shrugged. Jodie offered a weak nod in their direction and pulled her sunglasses down over her eyes. She felt nauseous from drinking too much coffee on an empty stomach and totally drained of energy. She'd watched them bond and now she was pulling them apart, like her father had done to her and Cole.

She pulled out her phone, distracted. *Where was Cole now?*

He hadn't returned from his appointment yet and she had no idea where he'd gone. One of the staff said he'd saddled up Pirate and gone out, even though he shouldn't have been riding after injuring his shoulder.

A laugh from the manège pulled her eyes away. Emmie and Toby were heading for the paddock, where Blaze was grazing on a fresh load of hay. Her heart lurched. 'Emmie, don't get too close,' she called.

She hadn't told her what had happened by the river. Yes, Blaze had shown a gentler side of himself to Cole, but he was still unpredictable. She crossed the grass towards them quickly, but Emmie was already standing on the fence, reaching a hand out.

'Emmie, be careful!' she warned, but she soon stopped in her tracks. Blaze had ambled over and gently rested his muzzle in her daughter's outstretched palm.

Emmie giggled. Jodie half expected to see Cole coming out of the stables. Maybe he was close by, making Blaze feel safe. But he was nowhere around. Her annoyance at him simmered.

He'd said in the meeting that he didn't want anyone but her taking over at Everleigh, but when she'd refused to commit beyond the year he'd gone AWOL. She didn't want to think he'd slept with her out of any ulterior motive, but he was acting like it now.

'Jodie!' Evie was crossing the garden towards her in her apron, holding two brown sandwich bags. 'For your supper.' The housekeeper beamed, plopping kisses to both cheeks and squeezing her shoulders warmly. 'I really hope you'll be back with us soon. It's been lovely having you and Emmie here.'

'Thank you so much, Evie.' Jodie hugged her warm, stocky frame, surprised to find tears in her eyes again behind her sunglasses. She wasn't prepared for this muddle of emotions.

'Where's Cole?'

'I don't know.'

Evie frowned, peering into the car as though she might find him hiding in the back seat. Jodie knew her face must have given her away as she sighed and placed the sandwich bags on the passenger seat.

'You know what he's like,' Evie said, lowering her voice as Emmie came running over to the car. 'He's always been better with animals than people. Keeps a lot inside, that one. But I *know* he thinks the world of you.'

* * *

The wind whipped Pirate's mane into the air like flames as the animal's muscles rippled under powerful legs, propelling Cole back towards the village from the cliffs.

He'd been trying to gallop away from the sense of self-loathing that had consumed him in the meeting and sent him into his usual fight or flight mode. Every time Jodie mentioned Ethan, he was reminded of how, divorced or not, their unconventional little family unit was her life. Everleigh wasn't. *He* wasn't.

He didn't deserve her as anything more than a business partner. He had no right expecting anything else to develop between them. But, then, he hadn't exactly been expecting to spend the whole night having sex with her on his living-room floor, making up for lost time. He sucked in the sky as he flew through the air, recalling her moans of pleasure as she'd put herself heart and soul into his hands. It had been impossible to deny himself, even though he'd known there would be consequences afterwards. She'd wanted it to happen…she'd started it, even…but he should have been stronger.

'Faster, Pirate, boy!' he yelled.

The feel of her after all this time…he couldn't stop reliving it. No one else had ever come close to fitting him like that. But Emmie was her life now. Edinburgh was her life.

It was clear that Jodie was intent on selling after the year was up, no matter what she felt, or didn't feel, for him. He'd hurt her too much in the past, pushed her too far away. To him, last night had felt like a reconnection, but maybe she'd seen it as closure.

For Emmie's sake, he had to make sure they both knew they could come back here any time without any underlying awkwardness.

'Mum!' Emmie's voice in the back seat brought her out of her gloomy thoughts.

'What's wrong?'

'Mum, is that Cole?'

Jodie slowed the car. They were right outside The Ship Inn. His horse appeared in her rear-view mirror, sending the gravel flying as her heart kicked into overdrive. Cole was galloping towards them under the clear sky, startling the cows with his speed.

Jodie held her breath. She flung the car door open, right as Cole dismounted in one jump.

'I'm sorry I got held up,' he said as his boots hit the ground. He clasped the reins in one hand and raked a hand through his windswept hair with the other.

'Were you trying to avoid me?' she asked bluntly, folding her arms. The breeze sent her hair flying out, tickling her face, and it reminded her of when they'd stood here on the day of the funeral, facing each other. A lot had happened since then. *What might happen in a year?*

He grunted and tipped his hat. 'I'm not great at goodbyes.'

'I already know that, Cole.'

Cole's very presence was making her heart race but she hoped her face didn't show it. She wanted to tell him last night had been a mistake, because it had been…they had to work together from now on. She couldn't put Emmie through any more drama, and she refused to put herself through any more emotional stress at the hands of this man.

His hands. She looked at them now, remembering the feel of his fingers in places they hadn't been for a long time.

She studied the mouth that had spent all night

exploring her and felt the shakiness return to her knees. The remnants of last night's actions lingered between them, bringing Cole to a stop almost at the tip of her now-scuffed boots, making him shove his hands into his pockets.

'Did you chase us all this way so you could tell me something?' she managed.

Pirate snorted softly through pink nostrils. Cole lowered his voice, and threw her into his shadow as he stood over her. She swallowed.

'I wanted to tell you I'm sorry about last night,' he said, glancing at the car to make sure Emmie couldn't hear. 'It went too far, Jodie. I know you have a lot on your mind, a lot going on, and this has all been a shock for both of us. We got…carried away.'

Jodie felt the impact to her heart like a horse had rushed up and kicked her. She hadn't been expecting that. He continued. 'If you're going to be spending more time here, as equal partners, we should probably keep things professional. Don't you think? I know Emmie has been through a lot with your divorce already…'

She bit her lip, but he was only saying what she'd planned to say herself. She took a deep breath. 'I one hundred percent agree with you.'

Cole looked taken aback. 'You do?'

She swallowed, maintained her cool. 'We were just two people giving in to their…biological urges. You're not to blame, I'm not to blame. We're two very different people now, Cole, with very different lives. From this point on we are colleagues, equal partners in creating a sustainable future for Everleigh over the next year, that's all.'

He nodded, adjusted his hat awkwardly. 'And we don't know what will happen after that.'

'We'll find a new partner for you,' she replied, 'I'll help you do that.'

He was quiet for a moment, nodding slowly and thoughtfully the way he did when his brain was working overtime and he didn't know how to express himself. Or didn't want to. *Infuriating.*

'I guess I'll see you soon, then,' he said, lingering on the spot.

She kept her arms crossed tightly, resisting the urge to reach for him, or yell at him. She wanted to do both. What was happening to her? 'I guess you will.'

Cole stepped to the car window and tapped

on the glass. Emmie rolled down the window in response.

'Emmie, look after your mother, she needs you,' she heard him say.

'I'm perfectly capable of looking after myself, thank you,' Jodie snapped, brushing past him and re-inserting herself into the driver's seat.

'We should get going, it's a long drive.'

Three weeks later

'It looks a lot like your dog has eaten something that she can't digest,' Jodie said to the harried-looking woman. Aileen shifted the unhappy Doodle on the table between them. 'We can see a foreign body on the X-ray here, but at the moment we can't tell what it is.'

'You can't tell what it is?' The woman looked annoyed.

Jodie frowned at the X-ray again. 'No idea. But we'll have to remove it for Ringo's safety.'

The woman sighed. 'Please, do whatever you have to do for Ringo. I have to run. Will you let me know once you find out what it is? I can't think what he could have eaten. We don't leave things lying around the house... Mind you, I've been away a lot lately, and I don't know if my boyfriend's been spoiling him.' She looked thoughtful for a moment, petting the dog's head.

'He'll be fine with us,' Jodie said, though she knew Aileen and Maxeen would be performing the op. She had to run out to pick up Emmie's iPad and take it to Ethan's new place. Apparently she had a video call with Toby at Everleigh and she'd left the essential item at home by mistake. It was imperative she log in on time.

Jodie thought it was sweet how much they'd enjoyed each other's company on the estate. Emmie talked about it non-stop. On the other hand, she was annoyed that Cole hadn't so much as picked up a phone, let alone tried to initiate a video call. She supposed it was up to her to let him know when she'd be back, as per their agreement, but his stony silence wasn't making the prospect any more appealing.

When Jodie returned to West Bow, the operation was still under way. With less than twenty minutes till the next appointment she poured herself a cup of coffee in the little kitchen and resisted the temptation to call Cole.

She was back now. Back at West Bow, where

she belonged. She was living her normal life, in her normal routine. She'd needed normality to come to her final decision without Cole clouding up her thoughts. She was going to sell her share of Everleigh, just like she'd told him and the solicitor.

Or was she?

She frowned. She couldn't quite stick to a decision. Emmie was talking about it like it was some sort of utopia, all the horses, the puppies, the lambs and the marshmallow nights round the firepit…and Toby. Maybe they just needed more 'normal', she thought. Just a couple more weeks to forget the way her heart had fogged up her head around Cole, and for Emmie to remember she was a city kid who hadn't even wanted to go to Dorset in the first place.

Normal is good, she reminded herself yet again, glancing at the 'normal' moody dark sky and cobblestones on the narrow, cramped street outside. A far cry from the changeable skies over Dorset and the mud-splattered pathways they'd walked and ridden down, she thought with a slight pang.

A far cry from the feeling of home she didn't want to feel in Cole's arms but still did.

'Everything went to plan,' Aileen said, bustling into the kitchen. She deposited her gloves in the bin on the way past. 'But I think Ringo's humans have another problem on their hands now.'

'What's happened? What did the dog eat?'

'A pair of lacy red knickers.'

'You're kidding?'

'Nope. I showed them to the client and she said they weren't hers. Then she stormed out, yelling into her phone. It's not a great way to find out your boyfriend's cheating, is it?'

Jodie grimaced. 'The poor woman.'

'Well…you know what they say about love,' Aileen sighed.

'What do they say about love?'

Aileen frowned. 'You tell me! You've been in a different world since you got back from Everleigh. Something to do with your horse whisperer, and inheriting your uncle's estate?'

Jodie winced. 'Is it that obvious?'

'Very.'

'I'm sorry.'

Aileen put a hand lightly on her friend's arm. 'Why are you apologising? A lot has happened to you lately.'

Jodie let out a long sigh. 'I don't even know. The inheritance is one thing. I mean, I'll have to spend a lot more time away from this place.'

'That's why you have all of us,' Aileen said.

Jodie nodded, grateful for her team yet again. She knew that was only half the issue, of course. 'I feel guilty, I suppose,' she admitted. 'And a little bit silly. I didn't tell you…but I went back to him.'

Aileen grinned. 'Now we're getting to it! Like, *back* to him back to him?'

'Several times,' she groaned, putting her head in her hands. 'In one night.'

'Wow.'

'Yes, wow. But then we both agreed it was a mistake.'

'And why was it a mistake? You're both single.'

'Emmie asked me questions in the car… things about me and Cole,' she said, running her hands anxiously along a stethoscope on the desk. 'I didn't really tell her much about our history, Aileen. She doesn't know I was with Cole before I met her dad.'

'I don't see why any of that matters. You were

faithful to Ethan when you were married, raising Emmie.'

'Yes…physically. But not mentally.'

'Jodie, you're only human.' Aileen looked exasperated. 'Don't beat yourself up, you're a great mum. Tell me about this man, please. What kind of romance did you *have* with this Cole guy? He seems to have quite the hold on you.'

'A big one.' Jodie looked defeated. Aileen was always blunt and she was glad of it. It was what she needed. 'But then he broke me to pieces.'

'There's always one that does that.'

'I know, and you swear you'll never let them anywhere near you again…'

'And then your raging hormones take over,' Aileen said knowingly. 'The insufferable consequences of human imperfections, huh? Animals don't suffer this problem.'

'I don't even know why I did it.' Jodie grimaced. 'I don't know what happens to me when I'm with him. It's not normal. I went there for Everleigh, but he *is* Everleigh.'

In a flash she was back on the riverbank, watching Cole go under. Then back in the cabin, seeing all the photos of them he'd kept for some reason. Maybe he hadn't been over her when he'd said he was. And if not, why had he called things off?

It was too confusing, but she could have lost him in that river and the notion still killed her. It was all too much to think about.

Aileen took her stethoscope and shooed her towards the door. 'Go.'

'Go where?' Jodie almost stumbled in her non-slip shoes.

'Go back to him again. Or at least clear your schedule and talk to Emmie first. She can handle the truth. You owe it to yourself to be happy, Jodie, and I've never seen you like this before. Everything's under control here.'

As she said it, a dog barked and a cat yowled loudly in the kennels, making Aileen jump and curse, and Jodie burst out laughing for the first time in days.

'Normal is boring, by the way!' Aileen called after her down the corridor.

CHAPTER THIRTEEN

'WILL YOU BE OK, staying with your dad?'

Emmie looked up over her bowl of soup. 'Why? How long will you be gone?'

'I don't know yet,' she replied honestly. 'I've booked time off from West Bow for the next week, so…'

'This is about you and Cole, isn't it?' Emmie asked. 'There's something going on with you two. I'm not blind, Mum. Why don't you want to tell me?'

Jodie's heart sped up. She'd been anticipating this, and had wanted to sit down with Ethan, but when she'd filled him in, Ethan had suggested it might be best just coming from her. She took the butter out of the fridge and then sat next to Emmie.

'Truth time,' Emmie said, dropping her spoon.

Jodie picked up a bread roll and started buttering it absently, feeling the heat prickle right up her arms. 'Uncle Casper left me and Cole equal shares in Everleigh in his will. The meeting we had to stay for, that was so we could talk about it and all the legal implications.'

Emmie just blinked at her for a moment. 'You own half of the estate?'

'Yes.'

She scraped her chair back on the kitchen floor. 'Isn't that worth…like millions? Can I tell people we're rich now?'

Jodie rolled her eyes. 'I didn't raise you to talk like that. But it's worth a lot, yes.' She shot her daughter a sideways smile. 'A *lot*.'

Her daughter's eyes grew as round as saucers. 'Mum! What the—'

'Listen.' Jodie discarded the knife, putting a hand out over Emmie's. 'The will states I have to go back there over the course of a year as often as I can before I can sell my half. I have to work things out with Cole, help him find someone else who can—'

'Why would you *sell*?' Emmie was looking at her like she'd gone insane. Jodie sat back in her chair as Emmie gazed at her imploringly. 'Mum, seriously, why you would sell your half of Everleigh? I thought you loved it there. It's amazing. I mean, I know I didn't want to go there at first, but that was before...'

'Before you met Toby?' Jodie raised an eyebrow. Emmie scrunched up her nose.

'What? No, Toby's cool, but the horses... Mum, the animals, the veterinary practice, all the stuff Evie showed me how to cook. I didn't watch TV the whole time I was there.'

'I noticed.'

'Can I come back with you?'

'No, not this time, you have school.' Jodie pushed her own plate aside, preparing herself. 'Emmie, there's something else.'

'Is this the part where you tell me something's going on with Cole?' Emmie grinned impishly. 'I knew it!'

Jodie felt her face flush. She'd deflected the questions up till now but she knew Emmie deserved the truth. 'Cole and I were together for a few years. We just...fell in love as kids, then it suddenly got serious when we were older.'

'OK.' Emmie put her chin in her palms, listening intently.

'But he broke things off when we were nineteen, before I moved to Edinburgh, and that's when I met your dad. There wasn't much of a gap between those relationships.'

Emmie's eyebrows shot up. 'Are you trying to tell me Cole Crawford is my real dad?'

Jodie laughed. 'Don't be ridiculous. Emmie, listen, all you need to know is I love you, and so does your dad. And I loved Cole for a long time before that. He just wasn't too hot at communicating with humans when we were together.' *He still isn't*, she thought, but she didn't say it. 'He's always been better with animals.'

'You mean you *love* him,' Emmie corrected her. 'I don't know what went wrong with you two, and I thank him for breaking up with you because it meant I was born. I am totally awesome…'

'Yes, you are.'

'But you still love each other. I've seen the way you look at each other when you both think the other isn't looking. And Toby said you spent the night with him before we left.'

Stunned, Jodie shifted in her chair, looking for signs of disgust or disdain in her daughter's blue eyes, but there were none.

Emmie was growing up so fast, she realised helplessly. She was losing the softness to her cheeks but getting tougher. She admired her daughter for the millionth time, even as embarrassment flared through her. 'I don't know what to say.'

Emmie smirked, rocking back on two chair legs. 'It's OK, Mum, we've had the sex talk at school.'

Jodie shook her head, biting back a smile. 'You're the best thing that ever happened to me, do you know that?

'Mum.' Emmie's eyes filled with love suddenly, a love so pure it shocked Jodie.

'We're not together now,' she explained quickly, wondering when her daughter had got quite so mature. 'I just wanted to let you know the situation with the inheritance, and everything that comes with it. There might be times when you have to stay with your dad and Saskia a bit longer.'

Emmie frowned. *Now* she looked disturbed, but thankfully not at the concept of staying with her dad more. 'You're not with Cole now? After you…? But you guys were so angsty.'

Angsty? 'Emmie, it's complicated.'

'Adults are always so complicated.'

'Well, you're going to be one soon enough.' She smiled.

Emmie rolled her eyes. 'So when are you leaving again?'

'Tomorrow,' Jodie said, opening her arms. 'Can I get a hug?'

'Can I get a promise that you'll keep your share of Everleigh, so I can tell my friends my mum has an estate in Dorset with horses?'

'Not just yet.' Jodie's insides twisted, remembering how she'd left things with Cole. To her surprise and relief, Emmie hugged her anyway.

Jodie had hoped she would be able to get through some of West Bow's paperwork on the train journey to Dorset, but her mind was a whirlwind as she stared out the window. She felt a pang of sadness over leaving Emmie. They'd been getting on surprisingly better since coming back from Everleigh the first time, but she couldn't pull her out of school. And as much as Ethan supported her, he adored spending time with Emmie. She didn't want to deny him that.

She'd told Cole that what had happened had been a mistake. He'd said the same thing. Rejection had seen her building her defences back up again, and he had done that too, perhaps. Neither of them had been particularly nice to the other when they'd said that awkward goodbye.

She knew it was for the best if they focused on the rescue centre from now on, and the plans for the estate going forward.

Yet here she was, watching the three hundred and forty miles speed past in varying shades of green, feeling nauseous at the thought of seeing him again. She was heading back to the man she'd sworn just weeks ago that she had no feelings for whatsoever. But it wasn't exactly indifference causing her butterflies.

She pondered Aileen's final perspective on the inheritance clause:

'Maybe that's why Casper left you both the property? Maybe he knew it wasn't too late to fix things between you and Cole?'

Jodie looked up at the drizzly sky. If that was it, he wouldn't be getting his wish. Emmie might love Everleigh more than Jodie had ever expected her to but it didn't change the fact that Cole was still a locked-up tower of secrets that infuriated her.

There was no way she could keep her share of Everleigh and work with him beyond the allocated time unless he started to communicate with her in the same open, trusting, honest way he seemed to communicate with his horses.

Twilight was settling on the paddocks by the time her cab rumbled down the gravel pathway. The lights were on in Cole's cabin and she could make out two cars outside. The Land Rover and a sedan she didn't recognise.

'Ms Everleigh?'

Toby's voice took her by surprise as she stepped out from the cab and paid the driver. He was hurrying towards her from the kennels with a puppy under his arm. She didn't recognise it from the litter they'd rescued, but he had probably found homes for Lucy-Fur and co., thanks to his and Emmie's social media efforts.

'Where's Emmie?' he asked her. His eyes were wide and hopeful behind his glasses.

'Sorry, Toby, it's just me this time.'

His mouth twisted in disappointment. 'She told me it would just be you. I was hoping she was planning to surprise me. This is one of the new puppies!'

'Cute,' she said, pulling her bag from the back seat.

'I guess you're looking for Cole. He has a client, but I can take you over there.'

'Oh, no, let's not disturb him,' she said as the cab crunched back up the driveway.

'He won't care. I have to feed Ziggy anyway. I always feed him when Cole has clients.'

Toby was persistent. He even carried her bag to the cabin porch. She followed him inside and the familiar scent of Cole, cleaning products and coffee filled her nose and made her empty stomach shift uneasily.

'Cole!' Toby called out as Ziggy made a beeline straight for her from the sheepskin rug by the fire, and started sniffing her ankles.

She heard Cole's voice behind the door to his consultation room, the extension he'd built onto the cabin where he saw his clients and their animals.

'One second, please, I'll be right back.'

The door was flung open and his deep voice pierced the air. 'Toby, hey, there's a new bag of kibble by the bench, thank you, buddy. Can you walk Ziggy too?' He stopped in surprise when he saw her. 'Jodie.'

She raised a hand awkwardly as Toby dropped her belongings on the floor by Cole's old weathered leather boots and went about fetching the giant sack of dog food. Ziggy padded after him expectantly.

'I left you a message to say which train I was getting. But I know you're busy. I can wait,' she said.

He'd shaved his beard off, she noted. He looked younger, like he had when he'd been nineteen, only there was muscle on him now, and biceps stretching out the fabric of a smart blue shirt. He looked good. Tired, but good.

She knew she didn't look great herself after a day of sitting on trains, but then again so what? He'd seen her look far worse. And she shouldn't even care what she looked like, it wasn't like she'd come back to romance him. She was here because Casper had given her no choice, and because she wouldn't have heard the end of it from Aileen if she didn't at least attempt to talk to him about some of the more personal stuff still left unaddressed.

'You're still going to sell,' he stated, stepping towards her.

She frowned. Trust him to get straight to

business now that she'd hurt his pride. 'I don't see why anything should have changed,' she told him, adjusting her handbag on her shoulder. 'Evie's fixed me a room in the house while I get to know the property a little better. I can shadow others here if you don't want me with you.'

He ran a hand across his chin then dashed it through his hair like he was trying to figure out what to do with her now she was standing here. He hadn't responded to the message she'd sent on the way here, but she could see his phone now, abandoned on the arm of the couch.

She heard the kibble hitting the metal bowl in the kitchen, right before Toby slid past them, flashed them a cheeky, knowing grin and slipped back out the door with Ziggy.

They were alone.

Her breathing constricted as Cole stepped closer, his brown eyes boring into hers. Without warning, he closed the space between them, brought a big warm, gentle palm to her cheek then ran a thumb across her lower lip.

'I definitely don't want you with me after what happened before,' he stated. His gravelly voice was almost a growl.

A maddening half-smile quirked his mouth before he lowered his lips to hers and pressed a kiss down possessively, like a stamp.

Jodie sank into him instantly, heating up at the thrill of his hands following the curves of her body and the hard spines of his prized books against her back. She couldn't recall how she came to be backed against the bookshelf. The passion overwhelmed her like it always did. She almost forgot where she was as she brought her arms around his muscled shoulders and her legs around his middle, losing herself in their kiss. She was losing her mind.

What was she doing? 'Cole!'

Quickly she broke free, scrambling breathlessly to pull her skirt back into place. She stepped back from him, hands to his chest as a barrier. 'I thought we said—'

'You're right, we did,' he interjected. He looked amused now, scanning her eyes. 'Old habits die hard. I guess you woke something up the last time you were here…so to speak. It won't happen again.'

She wanted to slap him but she'd kissed him too, hungrily, the way she'd been thinking about doing during the whole train ride, in spite of trying not to. 'Well, please make sure it doesn't,' she said, flustered, 'I'm serious, you know that's not why I'm here. Don't try that again.'

'As you wish.'

Cole stepped away like nothing had happened, leaving her colder. 'Meet me in the main house. I'll bring Miss Edgerton over to the surgery,' he said.

She blinked at him, bringing a hand up to her messy hair and smoothing down her skirt again. *What was happening?* 'Who?'

Without answering, he made for the consultation room and disappeared inside again, leaving her reeling. It was only then that she remembered he still had a client waiting.

CHAPTER FOURTEEN

ONE LOOK AT the bulldog bitch's quivering frame and bulging abdomen, and Cole knew the C-section couldn't wait. Blue was in the early stages of labour already and not happy about it at all.

'You got here just in time,' he told Jodie in the surgery, handing her a fresh white coat. It was dark outside now and he was on emergency call tonight, much to his chagrin. Or maybe it was a good thing, he mused. It would stop him making his way to Jodie knowing any more intimacy was off limits. 'Dacey finished her shift an hour ago, but this will take more than one pair of hands…'

'Usually one for each puppy, I know.'

'We'll do what we can. I hope you don't mind.'

'Straight in at the deep end, huh?' She smiled.

Jodie buttoned up the coat he handed her and he lowered his voice, glancing behind her at the woman who'd brought Blue in. 'About what happened back there, I really am sorry,' he said. 'I know we said that spending the night together was a mistake. I respect that you're here for Everleigh, I hope you know that.'

He was telling her the truth, but the sight of her in the cabin again had just rebooted his desires. He'd been thinking about her ever since she'd left, but he hadn't once pestered her for details about her return. He'd known he had to wait for her to come to him and she was bound to still have her guard up.

Jodie let out a sigh and he swore he saw desire in her eyes, along with frustration. 'I kissed you back. Let's just get to work, shall we?'

'Blue's owner didn't know most French bulldogs can only give birth by C-section,' Cole told Jodie, barely murmuring. 'She brought Blue in to me because the labour was going on too long, and she thought there might be something else wrong with her. The dog was trying to bite her before I stepped in, too.'

He watched Jodie fix her hair up in a quick bun. 'I've met plenty of people who don't know enough about the pets they choose to keep,' she said quietly.

He was glad she'd shown up when she had. He could handle things like this himself, he always had, but Jodie's presence and opinions were invaluable. She looked damn sexy too, all dishevelled after her train ride. Not that he should be thinking things like that. This was business now. Strictly business.

'So why can't she do this on her own?' the dog owner asked the second Cole and Jodie reached the operating table.

'Their hips are too small for them to do it naturally, Miss Edgerton,' Jodie said, pulling on a pair of latex gloves from the box he passed to her. The dog jerked her head suddenly, as if it was aiming for a bite at Jodie. It caught the end of the glove but no flesh, thankfully. Jodie pulled her hand away fast. 'Whoa, little one, we won't hurt you.'

Cole could tell the animal was fearful and wary, but judging by the animal's behaviour in this woman's presence it had more to do with the owners, unfortunately, than the pending C-section. Not that he was going to say that now.

He took a step back, one hand on the table, the other stroking the dog's velvety ears. Jodie's expression softened when the dog calmed in his hands and laid her head on his palm.

'I haven't seen her trust a stranger like that in a while. So it's true what they say about you.' The other woman was looking at Cole in mild suspicion.

'And what do they say about me?' he asked, signalling Jodie to administer the anaesthetic.

'They say you're a pet psychic.'

Cole felt his mouth twitch. People called him all kinds of things when 'vet' seemed too pedestrian for what they witnessed him do. He'd been called a counsellor, a therapist, a psychic, a healer, an animal whisperer and countless other things based on vague pseudoscientific theories. He didn't care for any title really; but it seemed to make people happy to give him one.

'What do you consider yourself, then?' Jodie asked him.

He thought about it, looking at her like the answer might be in the shape of her mouth in the surgical lights, the flecks of amber in the blues of her irises. 'I'm just a man. I don't do anything we can't all do if we choose to listen.'

Jodie smiled behind her hand as the woman frowned in contemplation. Cole wondered if

Jodie had told anyone what had happened with Blaze on the riverbank. He'd been making great progress with the horse but he hadn't expected that. Ziggy had surprised him too, leaping into the water after him.

Neither had surprised him as much as Jodie, however. Surrendering herself to him with such longing and passion, no wonder he hadn't stopped thinking about getting her back here. He had to smash her guard down more often, but he knew there were things he'd have to tell her about the past for that to happen. And those things from the past might end up turning her against him even more in the future.

'Sometimes it's better to get them spayed so they don't have to go through this,' Jodie was saying now, turning the woman's attention back to Blue as they laid the dog on her side. 'I'm surprised she's pregnant at all. A lot of Frenchies need artificial insemination.'

'My boyfriend brought the stud over,' the woman explained. 'He said we could make good money from the puppies. He lost his job at Christmas.'

Cole knew exactly what Jodie would say before she even said it. Sure enough, she crossed her arms and looked disparagingly at Miss Edgerton across the table.

'Putting a dog through this just to make some quick cash…'

'I know, it's not fair. I didn't know it would be so hard on her. We do love her.'

She produced a photo from her purse. They scanned it together quickly side by side. In it, the woman had her arm around a guy in his mid-thirties wearing bright blue trainers. The dog had her tongue lolling out between them.

'It's OK,' Cole said quickly. 'We're here now, and we're going to help her. It might be best if you waited outside, Miss Edgerton.'

Jodie gave him a look as if to apologise for speaking out of turn, but he wasn't about to make her think she should be sorry. She could say what she liked, she was entitled to speak her mind. People who loved animals weren't always the best owners.

'I can tell you something else about Blue,' he said some time later.

'What's that?' Jodie was inserting the last of the stitches to the Frenchie's belly. He watched her eyes with their blue laser focus.

He didn't usually say things like this to Dacey or Vin as he didn't want to compromise their own judgements or skills in training. But Jodie's bluntness with the owner was proof that she still trusted his instincts. 'I think the dog's been mirroring what's been going on at home.'

Jodie narrowed her eyesover her mask, intrigued. 'You think she's aggressive because someone else around her is aggressive.'

'Unfortunately yes. I've seen it a lot. I saw it in my own pets as a kid.'

'What do you mean?' Jodie looked confused and he cursed himself. But he'd started now. 'Well, you saw my dad drunk that time,' he said carefully. 'But that wasn't the first time. Animals pick up on unsettling behaviour. Sometimes even the chickens would act up if he went out there in the coop with too many beers in him. I had to learn pretty fast how to calm them down.'

He realised as he said it that his dad had driven him to discovering his special talents with the animals. In some strange way he was indebted to him for that as much as he was to Casper for nurturing them.

To his surprise, Jodie put a hand on his arm

and squeezed it. 'I had a feeling something else was going on at Thistles,' she said, with more compassion than he probably deserved. 'You never told me your father was an alcoholic. Is that why you never took me back to your house?'

He held her gaze as the shame roared through him again. It had been worse than his father being drunk most of the time, but of course he'd never got the chance to tell her that in person. It was all in the letter.

'Of course, I forgot, we don't talk about you, do we,' she said coolly, obviously disappointed by his silence. 'But I trust you to do the right thing for Blue. Do you want to talk to her owner together?'

He nodded, appreciating her all over again, not just her body, which he could rediscover every day for hours, but her inestimable capacity for her faith in him, in spite of the tension bubbling up between them again. He didn't want sympathy over his father, he never had, not from anyone. He simply saw it as his duty to help prevent another human or animal from having to endure what he had.

He knew she deserved some answers, though.

Maybe he should just give her the letter. Either way, they needed to talk. He was just as perceptive around Jodie as ever. There were things she wasn't telling him too. About Ethan.

When Blue was in recovery, Cole told the woman they would prefer to keep the dogs at Everleigh, where they'd be registered and licensed before being up for adoption.

'Will we still get to sell them?' She looked hopefully between them.

'We can't stop you claiming money for them, Miss Edgerton, as a hobby breeder,' Jodie said tactfully. 'But they'll get the proper treatment here while they're waiting for their new homes, and so will Blue while she's nursing.'

'Toby will find them homes in no time,' he added from across the room. He'd just checked his phone for new emergencies. None. *For now.* 'He's my self-appointed social media assistant. He and Jodie's daughter here have been finding good homes for all our animals through a social media account.'

The woman looked appeased, but Jodie was quiet as they cleaned up together afterwards.

'Did you know Toby and Emmie have been

in touch pretty much every day since we left?'
she asked him.

'I had some idea about that, yes.' He watched
her shake out her hair and unbutton her surgical coat, looking pensive for a moment. He
admired how protective she was over Emmie.
'It's not a romance, though. They're much too
young for that.' He slid up to the polished counter beside her. 'We'd know if it was.'

'I guess we would,' she replied tentatively,
shooting him a sidelong glance.

He kept his hands to himself, though they
itched to touch her again. He almost said their
lovemaking a few weeks ago had been the best
they'd ever had, and he knew she hadn't forgotten their encounter in the cabin earlier either.
Desire was written all over her face even now.
But he wouldn't make a move; he'd promised
he wouldn't.

He put his hands to the bench on either side
of her. 'I missed you,' he admitted. 'The last
three weeks…the last twelve years. You weren't
happy, were you, getting married? You looked
like you were in the photos, but you didn't love
Ethan.'

'Cole…' She met his eyes. 'Why do you care so much about Ethan?'

'I guess I care that there were things we both could have done differently back then,' he said.

She looked affronted suddenly. 'We? I don't regret having Emmie.'

He bit his cheeks for a second. 'That's not what I meant.'

'I'm tired of trying to read between the lines with you, Cole.' She tossed her coat into the laundry basket. 'It's been a long day. Can we pick this up tomorrow? We need to discuss things when we're in a better frame of mind— like who you'd like to approach as a potential partner for this place when I sell.'

He raised an eyebrow but didn't move from the counter. He wouldn't make a move, and he wouldn't react to provocation like this either. He had no intention of doing anything that might make her turn around and leave again. While she was here, he had to remind Jodie why this could be *her* home again, and Emmie's too.

'I'll see you in the morning, then,' he said. 'Bright and early. I'll make the coffee.' An idea was already forming in his head.

CHAPTER FIFTEEN

BLAZE'S WOUNDS HAD almost healed completely. The cuts and scrapes she'd seen before were nearly back to normal, giving the horse a new majestic prowess. 'He looks like a different animal,' Jodie said, sending out her silent gratitude for what Blaze had done to save Cole.

'He's coming around slowly.' Cole ran his hand over Blaze's forehead and muzzle. 'Russell can get closer now, without any trouble.'

'Not as close as you, I bet. How's his leg?'

'He's fine,' Cole said. 'He's strong. I wouldn't have hired him otherwise. Blaze won't be the only temperamental creature we have in here if the rescue plans work out.'

Cole hadn't mentioned the rescue centre in a while, but the thought of bringing it to life made her feel fuzzy and content, like a daydream she was nurturing, until she remembered everything she would have to uproot and change if she were to become a permanent fixture here.

Selling still seemed like a viable option, for many reasons, but Emmie kept messaging her, asking if she'd decided to keep it yet. Ethan had also asked again. She had a feeling he was getting more concerned than he was letting on, hearing Emmie rave about the place. She'd told him she was planning to sell, just as she'd told Cole. But every time she said it now it didn't seem to feel right. Especially on beautiful mornings like this.

The stable was warm and made her nose tickle with dry grass and anticipation. It was barely sunrise. They were loaded with coffee and a bag of pastries and she still didn't really know why they were going to Portland Bill. Cole had just said he had something to show her.

'You're not going to ride him, are you?' she asked suddenly. Cole was holding the reins up to Blaze, like he was measuring them to his face.

'He's not quite ready for that yet,' he told her. The bulk of him was reassuring beside her; he knew what he was doing, and she knew he'd never put her in danger. It didn't stop her worrying about him, though.

He might have broken her heart once but it pained her to know he'd had to deal with a drunken father as a kid, before he'd met her. Maybe even after that too… She frowned to herself. Come to think of it, she and Cole had only got together after his father had been locked away. And as soon as he'd got out, Cole had broken up with her. Something about it didn't add up.

'Evie told me she saw Emmie with Blaze, before you left the first time. Emmie could get close to him,' he said now, bringing her back to the moment. He was patting Blaze's long, sleek neck with a firm hand. 'Sounds like progress.'

Jodie watched the dust fly from Blaze's coat, remembering what she'd seen. 'He put his nose in her hand,' she confirmed, studying Cole's profile as he did the same, letting Blaze nuzzle his hand.

Cole looked impressed. 'He won't let anyone else do that yet, except me.'

Blaze wasn't wary of Cole at all any more, but as for her, she couldn't be sure. They had a couple of hours on horseback ahead to reach Portland Bill. Even though Blaze had displayed a couple of heart-warming changes in character since his chaotic, hostile arrival, Jodie didn't much care for the idea of taking such a temperamental stallion out on a long ride.

She watched as Cole seemed to pause time and space while he stood at the stall's gate, neither touching nor talking to Blaze.

After a moment Blaze lowered his head in what she took as submission and started munching on hay in front of her.

'I guess he's still a little self-conscious,' Cole said, turning to her with a smile. 'Maybe he considered himself a perfect specimen before the fire. Now not so much.'

She shook her head. 'He's still beautiful,' she said, without taking her eyes from Cole.

Jodie watched Cole during the whole ride towards Portland Bill, as the wind whipped their hair under the moody sky. She was back on Aphrodite. Cole was riding Jasper ahead of her like he owned the entire coast. It was clear that he belonged here.

Emmie would love being out on this ride right now, she thought, missing her already.

The rolling fields were like verdant green blankets, knitting into one as they galloped along the flower-strewn coast. When they finally dismounted, the rocky, windswept area around the lighthouse brought memories in with the waves. She was racking her brains now, trying to remember anything else Cole might have said about his dad. She drew a blank every time—he'd hardly ever mentioned him at all.

After his dad had got locked up, she'd thought maybe Cole had known what he had been doing all along. When she'd asked him that outright, he'd told her she was crazy and he'd seemed so affronted that she'd never mentioned his father again. He seemed to want it that way and she'd been so in love, so under Cole's spell she'd forgotten he'd had a father in jail at all.

Why was all this bugging her now?

At Portland Bill, Jodie tilted her head and tried to breathe in the sky as Cole walked the horses to a private paddock and tied the ropes around a giant post. It was covered in moss. The paddock hadn't been here before, she thought, taking in the fenced-off property around it. Apart from that it looked exactly the same. Casper had brought them here lots of times.

She trailed her gaze up to the red and white

striped tower. They'd taken the one hundred and fifty-three steps up to the top countless times as kids to look down in awe at the Jurassic Coast from the lantern room.

'Are you ready?' Cole came up behind her and looped his arms around her waist. For just a second she was thrust back in time, to when he'd done that every single day. The steadiness of him against her back in the wind took her breath away, then flooded her with fresh intrigue as he pulled a key from his pocket and dangled it in front of her.

On the tiny but shiny, expensive-looking motorboat, Cole steered them over the waves expertly. The wind tussled with her hair and the engine powered them over every wave bump, and Jodie appreciated Cole in silence, not least when he pulled her against his shoulder to shelter her from the wind. She didn't want to like the way that physically he made her feel so safe and protected, but she did.

'Remember when you told me which dinosaurs used to live around here?' she said into his shoulder, flashing back to them looking out together from the top of the lighthouse. 'I always pictured you taming a T-Rex, living amongst them all quite happily.'

Amusement played on his lips. 'I would have given it a go.'

He slowed the boat till they were bobbing gently on the blue. She took the seat opposite him and studied his muscles in the sunlight as he poured them thick hot coffees from a red flask. He was wearing a cream fisherman's knit sweater with the sleeves rolled up and clean jeans with the same brown boots. He might have even polished them, and Jodie found herself admiring the boat they were in. It was gleaming too, like whoever owned it saw it as their pride and joy. 'How long have you had access to that paddock and this boat?' she asked.

Cole sat back with his drink, stretching his long legs out between hers. 'I bought the boat about five years ago.'

Jodie raised her eyebrows. 'You own it?'

He slapped its side, like it was a stallion he'd broken in. 'Every last inch of fibreglass. I bought the land too, where I built the boathouse and the paddock. The plan is to put a guesthouse up eventually. I'll give people access to the boat and fishing rods, and we'll do rides along the coast… It's only a rough plan. But I have time. I'm not going anywhere.'

His eyes seemed to burn that last statement into her brain as he put the flask down at his side. 'Stop trying to make me not want to go anywhere either,' she muttered, so quietly she wasn't sure if he caught it.

He smirked, holding her gaze. 'Why would I do that?'

'You only want me to keep my half of Everleigh so some stranger won't come in and change things,' she challenged him.

He shoved his sunglasses up to his hair. She sensed the smugness fading, and a silent urge to prove something take its place before he reached across the gap for her hands. 'Come on, Jodie, you know that's not the only reason. Who are we kidding here? I was trying to do the right thing by you and Emmie, making this all less awkward. If you want to keep this strictly business we will, but I don't think you really want to.'

The wind caught his hair. The lighthouse loomed behind him. Before she knew it he was on his knees in front of her, making the boat rock. 'We have the chance to make something of this place together, like we always said we would.'

'I can't bring Emmie into this,' she told him as her heart skidded.

'Into what?'

'This!' She dropped his hands and indicated the salty air between them. 'I know you're still dealing with some stuff from the past, Cole, and you don't have to tell me what it is, but if you don't, it's always going to be there, between us. Was it something to do with your dad?'

Cole looked lost for a second. He sat back on the seat, drew his sunglasses down over his eyes and turned to the lighthouse, closing himself off again the way he always did. She wrapped her arms around herself, waiting.

He'd done so much without her. He'd made a name for himself and bought his own piece of Dorset. She had almost forgotten what it was like to feel this fire burn through her entire body and soul. She'd felt snatches of it over the years, enough to squish the silent longing for something more perhaps, but Cole was something else. Even his secrets kept her hooked. But it wasn't enough. She had to put Emmie first, above her urge to fall into him regardless of the issues that had kept them apart.

'You still won't talk to me?'

She could tell by the look on his face that she'd hit a nerve, or touched on something she wasn't supposed to know about. She continued, softer this time. Whatever it was that he didn't want to talk about had clearly affected him deeply and her heart went out to him suddenly.

'Look, I wouldn't have had Emmie if you hadn't broken things off with me, so how I can regret that, really? But you need to tell me what happened.'

'Dad refused to pay—or let Mum pay—for me to study in Edinburgh when he got out of prison, Jodie,' he said. 'And I didn't want you to waste your life waiting around for me in case I never made it.'

Her hand came up over her mouth before she had to grip the side of the boat again. 'Why didn't you tell me?'

'I didn't want anyone's help either, you know what I was like. I thought I could figure things out, but then you got pregnant and Casper told me not to go to you.'

The boat started rocking harder in the wind. Jodie's hair lashed her face but she swiped at it, zoning in on Cole. 'Wait… *Casper* told you that?'

Her knuckles were white. Her throat turned as dry as parchment. She felt sick, and not because of the sea, although it didn't help. 'Why couldn't you have come sooner?'

Cole looked anguished. 'I wish I could explain. It was a difficult time, Jodie. I thought you'd be better off without me.'

'Well, I wasn't.' Jodie couldn't stand it. 'Ethan and I had an agreement, Cole. His dad was on the verge of winning his constituency seat again, and he didn't need a teenage pregnancy right in the middle of his campaign. Ethan's and my parents offered us support to finish our degrees, but only if we married, so we made it legal and carried on with our studies too, but we always knew we'd get divorced once we graduated.'

Cole's fists were clenched. 'So you got married for some rich, upper-class guy's political gain.'

'No one forced me into anything, Cole. I was

just so in love with you I didn't care what happened to me!'

Cole crossed the boat on his knees towards her, at the same time she went him, and the boat rocked so hard she let out a shriek that dissolved in his mouth as they met in a kiss. He fisted her hair in bunches and her hands fumbled at the buttons on his jeans.

Then…

Over his shoulder, gulls were squawking, circling something under the surface. Jodie sprang away and sat up straighter. 'Cole, look!'

Dolphins' fins were skimming the water, one followed by another, then another, making a glistening whirlpool in the sunlight. She gripped the boat side in awe. '*This* was what you brought me here to see?'

Cole's eyes were fixed on the horizon behind his sunglasses, surveying the dolphins' frenzied swimming. They were starting to create a frothy white foam on the water. 'There's usually ten or eleven around this time of day,' he told her. 'They know this boat by now. I come out here to read. Normally they swim right over.'

Yanking his sweater straight again, he crossed the benches with two strides and crouched in the bow. Adrenaline flooded her as he took a moment to observe the situation. Then he gestured to the driver's seat, urging her to steer. 'Jodie, get us over there.'

The fishing net was tangled around the dolphin calf's nose and dorsal fin. There was no boat in sight but the net could have come in on the tide and cost this creature its life.

'Cole, we have to do something.' Jodie echoed his thoughts beside him. She was hauling the net in with him over the side, splashing ice-cold seawater all over herself as they tried and failed to raise the tangled dolphin higher.

Cole was fuming inside. This was something he'd never seen before. He would never have expected this around the lighthouse, these waters were supposed to be protected.

'Grab that box under the driver's seat,' he said to her when they couldn't raise the net any higher. 'The net's stuck on something, I need the knife.'

He figured the dolphin pod had been sending his boat a plea for help by not coming over to him, like they normally did. One or two were calves, including the one in the net, and the rest were eleven-foot adults. He knew them all by sight but he'd never seen them behave like this.

An adult female prodded the air with her nose, coming up alongside him and squeaking in earnest as he worked the oar to bring the net up to the surface. Her body language told him she was distraught; this must be the mother.

Standing up, he started taking off his shirt.

'What are you doing?' Jodie slid him the medical kit. 'It's too cold…'

'We'll have to cut the calf out of the net and we can't do it from here.'

'Then I'll do it,' she said, undoing her jeans quickly.

He put a hand on her wrist quickly, seeing the goosebumps on her arms. 'Jodie, you're not getting in the water.'

She pulled back in defiance, unbuttoning her shirt. The gulls above them were deafening. 'You need to be up here to help pull me up and steer,' she said. 'I'm smaller, I'll also dry quicker, but you'll have to keep me warm.'

'OK, *some* of that is logical,' he said, but in a flash she was naked apart from matching black underwear and kicking her jeans aside. She took the knife he was holding and stepped onto the seat. He was too distracted by what he was seeing to stop her jumping in. 'Jodie, you'll get tangled in the net...'

'It's OK,' she said, gasping for a second at the shock of the icy water. 'It's not that bad,' she lied.

The dolphins surrounded her. For a second he worried they might do something out of fear, but he knew they trusted him as he'd been coming here for a year or so, observing their behaviour while they were observing his. It was why he'd bought the boat. But he wouldn't let her do this alone, even though she thought she could.

He dropped the anchor quickly, made sure the tiny ladder was down in the water. In seconds, Cole was stripped bare and in the water beside her.

'Help me hold it, like this,' he said, coming up alongside her. The milky white of her flesh in the water could probably be seen for miles but she wasn't complaining if she was cold.

They had the net under control in seconds, but the poor calf was still struggling below them. They had to take it in turns to dive under with the knife and carve away at the nets for as long as their breath would last.

To his surprise, the dolphins started breaching and pirouetting around them and the boat. He forgot how cold he was as he took his eighth or ninth dive with the knife.

By the time the last tangle of rope was cut away, Jodie's lips were blue, but her eyes were enchanted when the calf wriggled free and swam around them. Cole tossed the knife back into the boat. He knew they were running on adrenaline, and he had to get them out of the water, quickly.

'Do you think she'll be OK?' Jodie asked, from the ladder. Her knuckles were white, her thighs and arms prickled with cold, but she still wasn't grumbling at all. He had never seen her look more beautiful than she was at this moment.

'She wasn't cut up…she was lucky,' he said, hitting the deck after her. 'And they'll stay away from fishing nets from now on.' He yanked at a pile of blankets and towels at his feet and cocooned her in them.

His brain was still swimming as he hauled the rest of the net up into the boat. It was heavy and his arms were tired. The ropes lashed his skin as he tossed them roughly under the bow.

He'd dispose of them where they couldn't cause any more harm. And he'd find out where those nets came from if it meant he had to call every-one he knew.

As he steered the boat, a squeal pulled his eyes from the horizon. The mother dolphin was following. She raced ahead and breached at the bow, sending a shower up over them and forc-ing Jodie to hide in her blankets.

'She's saying thank you,' he told her as she erupted into laughter. 'She knows you now. She knows you helped her baby.'

'We both did.' Jodie had stood up and was shaking against him with the cold as well as with laughter, and his arm looped around her, shielding her from the sea spray. The coast guard was coming up now. The car he'd called for was waiting up ahead already. He'd come back for the horses when Jodie was safe and dry.

Thanks to Jodie's quick actions and the dol-phin's trust in him, they had both changed the fate of that calf—he knew the pod wouldn't have trusted the coast guard like they did him, and they'd cut the net faster together anyway.

'The dolphins will never forget what just happened,' he told her, daring to hold her tighter and drop a kiss on the top of her head.

'Neither will I,' she said, and he almost told her he loved her, but he didn't. He'd already broken his promise not to make a move—not that she hadn't reciprocated.

They cruised towards the coast, which felt like coming out of a storm somehow, but Cole's adrenaline was still spiked hours later, after learning why she'd married Ethan.

The next few days of duties seemed to drag as Jodie went off with various media and staff members at Everleigh, and he continued with his appointments. He found himself looking forward to the next time the sound of her boots would echo out in the hallways, or her laughter would spill from the kitchen.

On the boat he'd told Jodie what she needed to know about his dad holding him back from going to Edinburgh, but somehow he hadn't been able to discuss the part about him being a lousy, abusive, violent man who'd threatened him with such terrible things. A cloud of shame for his former cowardly self seemed to follow him around permanently. He had never told anyone. What would Jodie think of him if he told her now?

All she had ever done had been to love him, but instead of protecting her from being hurt, like he'd tried to, he'd sent her straight to Ethan to be turned into some political pawn, manipulated by two sets of parents who should have known better.

CHAPTER SIXTEEN

THEIR DOLPHIN RESCUE off the coast made the news as soon as word from the coast guard got out, but Jodie hadn't told anyone why she'd jumped into the water first.

The truth was she'd panicked at the thought of Cole not coming up again, for whatever reason. She'd actively put herself first this time. The water had been freezing but she hadn't cared.

She'd almost told him she loved him as they'd sped back to land on the boat. Maybe she had still been high on adrenaline. The words had entered her brain and floated around, and made her heart ache to be heard, but they hadn't made it out of her mouth. She'd done enough to complicate things already.

She didn't want to press Cole for more answers about the past, but it was clear his pride had taken a hit over his family's dire financial status back then, and their wires had got crossed. And she hadn't exactly been honest with him before now about why she'd married Ethan. But she couldn't shake the nagging feeling that he was still hiding something else, that she might have only touched the tip of the iceberg.

Thoughts of what to do next with Emmie were still heavy on her mind. Jodie had to ask herself whether Everleigh really was the right place for Emmie if she decided not to sell.

One morning she paid a visit to Green Vale, Toby's school. He was giving a presentation to his class about the Everleigh animals.

'You're the woman who was with Cole Crawford and the dolphins! What brings you here today?' asked a woman in a yellow shirt bearing a nametag that said Hetty.

The main hall at Green Vale was a bustling dome, with seats made of straw bales. The kids all had fifteen minutes each for their presentations.

'I suppose I'm interested in seeing whether my daughter might…be a good fit here,' Jodie admitted to Hetty, watching the scene. She had been thinking about this progressive school more and more since Cole and Toby both spoke of the place so highly.

'My daughter is friends with Toby over there,' she told Hetty. Toby was getting ready to make his speech on the makeshift stage. She liked the vibe in the place already, people seemed happy. It wasn't like she'd had a chance to speak to Emmie about any potential long-term move to Dorset, she was merely looking around, garnering information to take back with her.

'Toby's a great student, love his energy. Did you see this, by the way?'

Hetty held out her phone to her. Jodie's throat dried up instantly. It was a photo, just posted on a local news site, of Cole's boat…way out in the distance, thank goodness. Jodie's face flushed. She could just make out the blurry shape of a man and a woman on board.

'Am I right thinking that's Cole Crawford's boat?' Hetty eyed her sideways. 'And I'm not being funny, because what you did for the dolphin was brave…but were you both naked?'

'Not quite—but it was the only way to help,' Jodie told her, as poised as she could manage it. 'Was that posted anonymously?' she asked.

'Looks like it. So you're a couple?' Hetty asked curiously.

'We're working together at Everleigh Estate,' she replied tactfully. 'I'm a vet.'

'Another vet! The perfect pair. He's a mysterious one, always keeps himself to himself. Everyone here's been wondering what kind of a woman would win his heart.'

Jodie didn't quite know what else to say, the woman was practically gushing over Cole. It annoyed her as much as it amused her.

The boat was too far away from the camera to tell for sure if they were clothed or not in the photo. She'd already spoken to a reporter herself, but it made her slightly uncomfortable knowing someone else had taken a photo like that and published it.

You couldn't make out any details, she reassured herself as she excused herself and took her seat.

She tried to focus on Toby and his puppy plan. They had a lot of puppy photos on the social feed suddenly, and Cole had taken a call last night about another rescue horse. Things seemed to be picking up again after Casper's death.

Over the course of the next year she and Cole would work together with the contractors and local land management to build more shelters and stables, hire more staff—technicians, vets, another receptionist and an office manager just for the rescues. Jodie knew Cole would happily start as soon as possible—he'd even brought it up as they were both so encouraged by their progress with Blaze.

But while she had given her go-ahead to the plans, she couldn't commit to being on the ground herself yet, not until she'd spoken to Emmie and Ethan. And as for her and Cole...

What *were* she and Cole now, apart from partners in Everleigh? The rumour mill was spinning but they seemed to be playing a dangerous game, tumbling into each other then taking a step back to process. He was giving her space, no pressure, but the more he did that, the more she wanted to pounce on him again.

'This is how Cole Crawford gets a horse to stop bucking.' Toby's voice jolted her out of her thoughts. A video of Cole was up on the screen, larger than life, as though she'd just summoned him.

From the looks on the parents' faces, Jodie

had a feeling most people in the area already knew about Cole's unique gifts. She felt another flutter of pride in her belly and couldn't help but smile. The kids were engrossed—they clearly all loved animals here, just like Emmie did.

When the presentations were over, she headed for Toby. 'Cole would be proud of you,' she said, taking the wriggling six-week-old beagle-cross puppy from his hands.

'I *am*...very proud.' Cole's voice behind her made her spin around.

'Have you been here the whole time?' she asked him in surprise, noting Ziggy at his feet. People around them were already recognising him, milling around like he was some sort of handsome celebrity. Hetty was staring from the lemonade stand, trying to make it look like she wasn't.

Cole cleared his throat. 'Came in a few minutes late. Sorry, had an issue with a lamb out by Abbotsbury.'

He gave Toby a high five then slung his arm around Jodie's shoulders, making her freeze in shock. 'I loved watching your face, when you saw the video of me,' he whispered in her ear, so discreetly that only she could hear.

In spite of her fluttering heart she held the puppy close and joined in with Cole making polite conversation with the people all around them. He hadn't touched her in public before now, not even in the farmhouse kitchen. If he was trying to make a point in front of everyone or create some more public buzz around them to stop her selling up and leaving a spinning rumour mill in her wake...she should have cared, deeply. She should have been offended. She was only here for Emmie—wasn't that obvious?

But to her surprise it *was* starting to feel good, his steady presence, the way he was opening up to her. Not enough perhaps, but little by little. There were things only she knew about Cole Crawford. And things only he knew about her.

She reminded herself she shouldn't care if they'd been seen out there at Portland Bill together, or anywhere else. It was no one's business but hers...but she still couldn't help wondering who'd taken the photo.

CHAPTER SEVENTEEN

IT WAS THREE-TEN a.m. when Jodie woke with a start. She was in Cole's bed and for a second she allowed herself to feel good, not guilty, about how a cosy fireside dinner in the farmhouse had somehow ended with them tearing each other's clothes off again in the cabin. Then she saw his side of the bed was empty. Cole was gone.

The candle on the hearth had burnt out. Lambing season meant all kinds of call-outs at odd hours, so she wasn't alarmed at first...but then she saw the flashlight outside through the window. The beam across her face had woken her up.

Jodie's heart surged as another light flashed fast across the flowers in the window. It seemed to be moving towards the kennels.

Grabbing up her phone, she sprang from the rug Cole had draped over her and pulled on his oversized shirt and her jeans, which they'd left on the couch. Her boots felt rough without her socks as she slid her bare feet into them. Outside, the dogs were strangely silent, which didn't feel right. Some of them always barked, unless it was someone they knew.

'Russell?' she called, expecting the stable-hand to answer. Nothing.

She shone her phone light into the night. 'Toby?'

She swallowed her nerves. It couldn't be Toby: he'd be in bed. Cole's Land Rover was gone from the driveway, so it definitely wasn't him either. It was just her, facing a row of quiet kennels.

She called Cole's phone, left a message. 'Cole, everything is probably OK, but I thought I saw a flashlight near the kennels. I came outside to check it out but…there's no one there. It's a bit weird.'

Embarrassed, she hung up. She didn't need to bother him over nothing and he was probably busy. She couldn't see anything out of the ordinary now, but she crossed the yard to the stables, just to check. The grass crunched under her feet. Inside, the horses were quiet. Some were sleeping, some were munching and she lingered a moment by Blaze.

'How are you, beautiful boy?' she whispered, breathing in the heady scent that always soothed her. The horse snorted softly but didn't move or show any agitation. She reached out a palm to an inch from his forehead. 'You can trust me,' she said.

To her surprise, Blaze lowered his head, if only slightly, permitting her to lay her hand flat against him. It was the softest touch, the first time she had ever touched him. Her heart thrummed this time with excitement as she stroked his face, around where his scars were healing well. She couldn't wait to tell Cole.

A noise made Blaze's ears prick up. Jodie raced back outside. It sounded like something heavy had fallen and now the dogs were barking up a storm. Back at the kennels she hovered in the shadows. 'Who's there?'

A black figure slipped behind the last cage in a row of kennels, where they kept Blue and her puppies.

'I'm calling the police!' she announced, as her heart leapt to her throat.

A light flickered on in the main house behind

her, just as the figure in black appeared right in front of her. Heavy hands slammed her against the bars of the last cage. Her phone shattered on the concrete. The impact across her back felt like someone had struck her with ten baseball bats and was so painful she lost her voice.

Gasping for her breath, Jodie kicked at the man pinning her by the shoulders, but he was strong for someone so slight. He was in his mid-thirties, wearing a black tracksuit and blue trainers. *She recognised those trainers...* 'What do you want?'

His clammy fists gripped her wrists. Jodie's brain was in overdrive. She thought she'd seen him somewhere before, but she couldn't place him. 'Let go of me!'

'Not unless you promise to be quiet.' His growl was pure alcohol. 'I'll be out of here in seconds, then you can just forget about me. Understood?'

Headlights suddenly roared towards them on the driveway. Her attacker faltered and Jodie watched the satchel he was holding slip from his shoulder. A car door slammed, a puppy yelped from inside the bag before a little head poked out—one of the French bulldog pups. 'Don't say a word,' her attacker warned her.

'Don't threaten me. You were trying to steal the dogs!' Struggling again to free her wrists, she almost kneed him where it would have hurt most. She got so close she could see the anticipation of impact in his eyes…but in a second he was gone, ripped from her at gunshot speed.

'Get away from her!'

Cole was here. A rush of air felt like a whiplash as he slammed the guy up to the bars with one arm and held the other across her like a barrier. 'What did you *do* to her?' he roared.

Jodie gasped and struggled for composure as Ziggy leapt around their feet. She tried to take hold of Cole's arm but he wasn't letting the man go. 'Cole, he didn't do anything. I'm OK.'

She watched his jaw tense as fury ravaged his features. His knuckles were white. A siren wailed briefly in the distance. 'Were you trying to take those dogs?' Cole's fury was pouring over the intruder like magma as she scooped two puppies up from around her smashed-up phone. Her legs were shaking in her boots.

'I was just taking what's mine!'

'What do you mean, what's yours?' Jodie

managed, but she remembered now where she'd seen those trainers. 'Cole, he's the guy from Miss Edgerton's photo...'

'I told my girlfriend she shouldn't have left them here with you!' The guy was fuming but Cole ignored him.

'Are you OK?' His eyes were slits of black, shimmering in fury and contempt. It shocked her.

'I'm fine.' Her back throbbed as she pickeded up the last pup. Cole saw her struggling a little on her feet, and the sight made his mouth contort before he hauled the guy into an empty kennel.

He swiped the bars across, bolting the iron gate shut. 'Stay quiet, you're on camera,' he snarled, jabbing one finger to the hidden security cam inside one of Ziggy's old dog toys.

He turned to Jodie and held her at arm's length. 'You're hurt.'

'Maybe a little bruised, but I'm fine. I'll be all right.'

Cole scanned her face like she was a precious jewel about to crack. Jodie's back was still throbbing but she knew it was nothing serious. She was just glad the man hadn't got away with his crime.

'I would have kneed him in the privates if you hadn't got to him first,' she told him. 'You came when you got my message?'

Cole's nostrils flared, and for a second he looked like he wasn't even there behind his own eyes. He was someone she didn't recognise at all.

'Cole?'

The police car was pulling up next to the Land Rover and double headlights shone accusingly on their locked-up perpetrator. Russell ran towards them, a policewoman close behind.

Cole seemed to retreat into himself as he strode down the line of kennels, somehow silencing the barking dogs in seconds. She noticed a shower of dog treats on the floor around the kennels. The perpetrator had stopped them barking by giving them food—the preparation was impressive for a drunk.

It transpired the man—John Kowara—had been following Cole, working out his schedule, planning on when to take the puppies back so he could sell them himself on the black market for a disproportionate price.

'It could have been him who was watching us from the lighthouse with a camera,' Jodie told the policewoman, hugging her arms around herself.

'We'll check his phone when we get to the station,' the policewoman told her. 'Meanwhile you should think about pressing charges for assault.'

'Yes, you definitely should,' Cole said through gritted teeth. His arm tensed around her shoulders as Kowara was carted away to the police car.

Later, in bed, she listened to the sound of Cole's steady breathing like a lullaby she'd missed for longer than she could remember, but Jodie still couldn't sleep. The scene kept playing on a loop inside her head—the attack, the residual shock of it, the poor pups, who must have been terrified, and Cole... Cole had gone crazy seeing her being threatened by that guy. He'd looked haunted more than anything and it was haunting her now. She had never seen anyone look like that in her life.

Cole passed the kennels, raising his hand in greeting at Toby, who was sweeping the cages eagerly like he did every Sunday morning. They had three more people coming to look at adopting dogs later and another crazy day ahead, enough to keep him and an army busy, but he couldn't stop his brain rehashing the break-in.

He'd just watched the security footage. Twice. It made his blood run cold, seeing Kowara making a lunge for Jodie.

Jodie and Dacey both looked up when he walked into the kitchen, and a little lamb wobbled out from around the fridge, knocking a magnet off the front as it passed.

'Did you watch it? Can you see him taking the puppies?' Jodie's eyes were brimming with concern as Dacey left the room to greet a client in the surgery.

He dodged the lamb and retrieved the magnet. 'It's all on film,' he said, sticking the photo of Evie's grandkids back on the fridge. 'It's with the police report.'

'OK…good. Well, if they need me, I can talk to them from the road.'

The sudden tightness in his chest made him put his coffee cup down without pouring anything. Jodie had to be at the airport in a matter of hours. She had been here just over a week already. He still didn't really know when she'd be back at Everleigh. It depended on Emmie's school and her ex's schedule, he supposed. He didn't want to pressure her by asking, especially after last night.

She probably *wanted* to go back. She'd been in danger here. He had put her in danger. He'd gone out on a call with Ziggy and he hadn't locked the door of the cabin behind him. Something far, far worse could have happened to Jodie after Kowara had scaled the fence at the entrance and sneaked in while she'd been sleeping to get the keys to the kennels.

Jodie crossed to him. 'Cole, are you OK?'

He glanced at her hand on his arm as his guts twisted up into a knot. 'It will be easier to press charges if they find evidence he was watching us before he broke in,' he said, picking up a chunk of ham from Evie's chopping board and tossing it to Ziggy.

'I probably won't press charges myself,' she announced suddenly, folding her arms.

She couldn't be serious. 'He attacked you, Jodie. You have to press charges.'

'He's already being prosecuted for theft and you got to him before he could do anything worse. Not that he would have done, he was just trying to scare me into letting him take the dogs. I told you, I was about to knee him where it hurts.'

Cole just stared at her, raking a hand across his chin, then shoved his hands in his pockets so she wouldn't see his fists clench. He'd been picturing his father the whole time he'd been staring at the footage. Kowara could have been him, laying his filthy hands on Jodie. It had brought everything back, the way he'd had to fight his father off, time after time.

'You don't know what he would have done to you, Jodie,' he growled. 'He was totally wasted.'

She poured herself a glass of water from the sink, sighed. 'I don't want to think about it, Cole. I have to get back to Emmie. I'm too busy—'

'Too busy?'

'Yes, and if we start that process we'll have to keep on thinking about it! Everything is OK now, isn't it? The police won't let it happen again and neither will you.'

His jaw clenched. The security footage still wouldn't leave his head. There was Jodie, wearing his shirt out in the yard. One second she'd been shining her phone around the kennels and the next she'd been pinned against the bars. It had made him see red. It had been his childhood all over again. He'd been the victim so many times, too damn scared to bring the man to justice; thinking he'd be hurt even more just for speaking out.

'I can't let you go without facing this, Jodie, and I'll be with you.' He wanted to rewind real time like he'd rewound the security footage, but he couldn't go back and stop Jodie being attacked on the property. *Their* property. She'd been adamant on selling her half before…she'd be even more determined to do so now. At least, he wouldn't blame her if she was.

He couldn't believe she just wanted to forget about it. Maybe she was frightened of the consequences of pressing charges, like he'd been all those years ago, fending off the fists that had always come at him.

'I told you, I'm OK. Please, just let it go,' she said gently, as if she was reading his mind, God forbid.

'I can't do that.'

Vinny came into the room with a bottle and took the lamb over by the fire for a feed. 'We have two kids and pigeon in there,' he said to Cole, nodding towards the surgery, oblivious to their conversation.

'I'll go and help. You rest,' Jodie said quickly, like she was trying to escape him. Cole followed her to the door.

'It's your last day and I'm not letting you out of my sight,' he said, keeping his voice low. Already it felt like she was slipping through his fingers.

She turned, eyes narrowed. 'Cole, you do know that what happened last night wasn't your fault? If anyone is to blame for him getting in, it's *both* of us. We were both distracted, doing things last night that we'd said we wouldn't do...'

'That's no excuse for what he did to you, Jodie.'

'You don't have to worry about me.'

But I do, he thought to himself, holding the door open, resisting the urge to reach for her. *I always worry about you, I always did everything I could and I still couldn't protect you.*

Jodie was downplaying her injuries and the shock of what had just happened to her to save *his* feelings, but he knew when she was hurt, inside and out. He spotted her stretching out her back a couple of times as she pulled her white coat on. She caught him looking, pretended she was fine. Just like he always used to do in front of her.

It was too late for pretence. He'd seen the bruises on her flesh in his bed this morning, angry black and blue marks along her spine. She was leaving Everleigh for Edinburgh hurt today, and that was everything he'd always done his best to prevent.

CHAPTER EIGHTEEN

THE TWO YOUNG boys studying the pigeon with Cole were a little older than Emmie and Toby, but it turned out they went to the same school. 'What happened here, guys?'

'We were playing in the field when we saw it. We think its wing is broken,' one of them said despondently.

The pigeon was silent in Cole's steady hands on the table. He held it up, showing them the tag on its bony pink leg. 'It's a racing pigeon. We can find out who set him off on his flight if we type this tag number into a special website.'

'Really?' The kids looked fascinated. Cole offered them seats so they could watch them at work, and their presence in the room eased Jodie's thrumming heart.

She was worried about Cole after last night. He blamed himself for leaving the door to the cabin unlocked so Kowara could help his sticky fingers to the kennel keys. It creeped her out, thinking how that guy must have seen her lying in bed, sleeping. Cole was driving himself crazy over it, but she didn't blame *him* for it.

'You were right about the broken wing,' Cole said to the kids as she set about cutting a twelve-inch strip of bandaging tape.

He folded the bird's wing against the side of its body in its natural position. The poor little thing kept turning its head and clucking as if it was searching for Cole's eyes, seeking comfort.

'Now we wrap the tape around the bird's body, which will hold the wing in place,' Cole explained to the boys, looking towards her for the tape.

She picked up the iPad to check the tracking number on the tag. 'Turns out it's from Cambridge. I'll give them a call and see what they want to do,' she said.

Sitting on hold with the Royal Pigeon Racing Association, her back felt uncomfortable again, but she wasn't about to let on and worry Cole. It was just bruised. He gave instructions to the kids if they wanted to look after the pigeon a while but, still, she could feel him watching her like a hawk, as if he was scared to let her out of his sight for more than a second.

Jodie glanced around at the oak-panelled walls and Casper's certificates, and the paddocks through the windows, where Blaze was trotting around. The sun was shining and spring was taking a firm hold—it seemed like for ever ago that they'd arrived in the snow.

Everleigh had always meant surrounding themselves with excitement, one way or another, good and bad, she thought. Things were no different now but her ties in Edinburgh were too tight for her to be on the ground here at Everleigh any longer.

Right now, it wouldn't be fair to anyone to commit to coming back in person, least of all Emmie. But already the thought of leaving Cole for any undetermined length of time was making her heart flap in her chest like another pigeon was stuck inside.

She wouldn't tell him but the image of Kowara's face bearing down on her against the bars of that kennel was getting harder to block out. She didn't want to sleep alone tonight back in her bed in Edinburgh, but she had no choice.

Cole stepped into the pen, flipping the latch back behind him. Jodie was stroking Blaze along his mane and he couldn't believe his eyes. She turned to him and shrugged, seeing his look of surprise.

'Didn't I tell you Blaze let me touch him last night, when I came in here?'

He frowned. 'When?'

'When I came into the stables to check these guys were all OK. I heard Kowara from here—' Jodie stopped what she was saying abruptly, like she was afraid to bring it up again.

'Maybe he'll be ready to ride sooner than you thought,' she said. He could tell she was desperate to change the subject.

'Only for someone he trusts,' he told her, taking her hands and drawing her close by the waist in her city-girl dress and sweater. She was dressed for somewhere else already; her boots in the hay were even shiny again. The thought of her suffering at all back in Edinburgh because of him made him feel sick to his stomach, even as he fought to transmit composure.

'I know last night affected you more than you're telling me,' he said, eyeing the saddle on the fence. They'd agreed to try and saddle Blaze before she left but he had other things on his mind now.

'I told you, I'm fine.'

'You're so stubborn.'

'Pot, kettle, black.'

They were waiting for her car. Her bags were all packed up outside, and he had no idea when he'd see her next. All he knew was that she'd be out there thinking about John Kowara and what he'd done…and how *he* hadn't been there to protect her. It would hit her eventually, when she got home.

'I want you to press charges,' he said firmly.

'This again?'

'You don't want to because it's not very nice to think about, but people like that need to get what's coming to them, Jodie. What if he hurts someone else?'

She pulled her hands away. 'What's wrong with you, Cole? Is this to cover Everleigh's reputation, because you think I'm still going to sell my half?'

'I don't care about that, I care about you!' Infuriated, he pulled the envelope from his jeans pocket. 'There's something I haven't told you.'

Blaze grunted behind them, sending dust clouds into the rafters. Cole knew he was picking up on his mood. He urged Jodie out of the pen by her hand, and shoved the letter into her other palm, ignoring the pounding in his chest, the foreboding feeling creeping like a freezing river around his body.

'I saw this before, with the photos, by your medicine box.' Jodie turned the envelope around in her hands, studying the red wax seal.

'Read it,' he ordered her. 'Maybe then you'll see why you need to press charges.'

Jodie's heart was like a leaden weight in her chest. She could barely finish the letter through the tears in her eyes. It was true, Cole had been coming to get her, and Casper had stopped him, but that wasn't it.

I told myself when I broke up with you that I was doing the right thing. I thought I was saving you from worrying about me, or getting yourself involved in any of my family's mess...

'Oh, my God!' she cried, looking up at him. The sun was streaming onto his hair and the wisps of grass and hay stuck to his jacket but it was like looking at a stranger now. Her fingers were trembling around the piece of paper.

'All those years I thought we'd told each other everything, I thought you'd let me in. But all the time you were keeping secrets, lying to me about how you got all those injuries. You were suffering all that alone, Cole? You didn't even trust me to try and help you?'

Cole's eyes widened then narrowed. He stepped towards her but she held up her hands to stop him.

'Jodie, I didn't let anyone try and help me. I thought I was protecting you.'

'You were the one who needed protection, Cole! He ruined us…and you just let him!'

She was so incensed she almost fell over her bag at her feet. The cab was coming to take her to the airport, and it couldn't arrive fast enough. The thought of how things could have been so different if he'd just opened up to her was suddenly all too much. 'You should have let me make up my own mind whether I needed you to protect me.'

'I knew you'd have gone to him, tried to defend me!'

'Damn right I would. I'd have done *something*, because I loved you so much.'

She could hardly think about what she'd read,

or the fact that she was only just learning this now. Cole looked like a restless rescue horse with nowhere left to run.

'I understand you didn't want to see me hurt but *you* hurt me, Cole, more than your father or Kowara ever could. Do you have any idea how long it took me to get over us? You let me think you didn't love me! You would've rather lost me…us…your education…your whole life, Cole, than confide in me so I could help you make a call to put your father back in prison where he belonged.'

The cab was pulling up. It was just like twelve years ago, she realised, when she'd driven off after a monumental row. But surely that day could have been prevented if he'd just told her the truth back then. 'I need to process this,' she said, and this time her voice came out as a croak. Part of her knew she was being unfair, but she couldn't help how she felt: sick with the knowledge of what he'd suffered at his father's hands but devastated that he'd kept such corrosive secrets from her for so long. Secrets that had ruined their relationship.

Cole's cheeks were pinched. He looked pale and angry. 'I know it's a lot to take in, but you must see now why you have to press charges, Jodie.'

'Yes, I do. Because *you* didn't, back when it mattered. Your father died before he could face any justice for what he did to you, and us! But what I do now won't change that, Cole.'

'Maybe not, but you can do it for Emmie.'

She flinched. 'Emmie? Emmie will never come back here now and neither will I.'

She pressed a hand against her mouth to stem the sobs the second his face broke into a dark scowl. He wasn't seeing anything from her perspective, even now. She could tell. He was still stewing over his own cage of secrets. Would he even have told her if she hadn't been attacked by Kowara? Love couldn't flourish where there was no trust.

'You're impossible, Cole.' She grabbed her bags, threw them into the back seat of the car.

'Airport,' she told the driver. And this time she didn't look back.

CHAPTER NINETEEN

One week later

'PENNY FOR YOUR THOUGHTS,' Ethan offered, sliding onto the leather chair opposite the sofa and putting his feet up on the coffee table.

'Does Saskia let you do that?' Jodie quipped from the posh leather couch and Ethan pulled a face then removed his trainers. Jodie laughed. She was at Ethan's new place, waiting for Saskia to bring Emmie back from a shopping trip. Jodie had made restaurant reservations for herself and Emmie close by, but she wasn't really in the mood.

'I don't know if my thoughts are worth a penny right now,' she said miserably.

Ethan pulled a mock frown. 'Are we still feeling mortified for flying off the handle at Cole?'

She groaned. 'OK, yes, I know I was way too hard on him, considering what he went through.'

She'd done a lot of reading on domestic violence in the last few days, and had discovered the hold abusers often had on their victims. He'd kept all that inside whilst caring for others, pouring out his compassion without measure yet never knowing how to ask for it himself, not even from her—not until he'd asked her to press charges against Kowara. Cole must have felt he'd had no choice but to let her go back then, and she'd just screamed at him selfishly for ruining *their* plans.

'Have you pressed charges against that guy yet?' Ethan eyed her sideways, just as Jodie's heart went haywire. He'd struck at the heart of the matter, as usual.

'I know I should,' she replied with a sigh, rummaging in her bag to find her ringing phone. It wasn't Cole. But, then, it never was. The two of them seemed to have reached a stalemate of sorts since she'd left Everleigh.

'It's getting to you, Jodie. Or maybe it's Cole, hmm? You told him you wouldn't ever go back there but you know you want to. You obviously still care about him.'

She stared at her manicure, wishing Ethan didn't know her so well. She'd told him everything. The two of *them* had never had any secrets. Sometimes she wished they were in love, instead of just being co-parents and best friends. She told him so and he smirked.

'You know, Emmie doesn't stop talking about that place.' He reached for her hand. 'I can't imagine why, but sometimes I think she'd rather be there than here, even with my giant plasma screen TV! Did you see my organised T-shirt drawer, by the way?'

She laughed again. He was being sarcastic, but Saskia's living room was catalogue perfect, and Jodie couldn't help imagining what she'd do if a lamb or chicken waddled across it like it might at Everleigh. She'd got used to the buzz and muck and mayhem of Dorset life yet again, and everywhere else felt too quiet now.

'I wouldn't want to take Emmie away from you, Ethan,' she told him. 'We raised her together, we went through all that nonsense our parents dished out together. We promised to always live close by, put her through school, college together...'

Ethan tutted. 'You wouldn't be moving her to Mars, Jodie. Besides, I quite like the thought of a little riding holiday in Dorset myself every now and then. Do you think Saskia will let me go?'

'If you keep putting your nasty feet on her coffee table I should think she'll pack your bags for you.' Jodie smiled. Ethan squeezed her fingers in solidarity. She should have known he would be fine with whatever decision she made about Everleigh: he was a good man.

It had been Cole as much as Ethan and Emmie's tight bond here that had been holding her back in her head. She'd created enough barriers herself to protect her own heart, and the more days that passed without him now, the more she regretted overreacting to his letter.

The security footage *had* been pretty shocking, she'd seen when she'd summoned the courage to watch it. It felt like she'd been watching someone else, not herself. Cole's fury at Kowara and then at her for not pressing charges had been a direct result of the pain he still harboured inside from his father doing the same thing to him. She couldn't bear the thought of him being hurt…all those cuts and bruises he'd tried to cover up.

The thought of how she'd left him flooded her with guilt all over again. She knew she should press charges for Cole as much as for herself and Emmie—and for the Cole she'd *used* to know, who'd lived in anticipation of his father's despicable, violent whims...

She should do it for Cole and for everyone else who'd ever been attacked or abused or violated like that. He had lied to her for so long only because he'd been afraid.

'When will you see Cole next?' Ethan asked in interest, but his phone was ringing now. Ethan answered, and the look on his face made her gasp.

'He's sick? How sick?'

'Who?' she mouthed, but Ethan was already grabbing both their jackets on the way to the door.

Cole hadn't been planning to go to The Ship Inn for the three-hundred-year anniversary party, but he thought it would be a good way to answer some of the questions the locals had been choosing to call him.

The recent media interest about the dolphin had got people talking, but at the party all people seemed to be interested in was him and Jodie.

It still made his fists curl to picture that guy's hands on her. The thought of her experiencing even the slightest bit of what he'd felt when his father had been loaded on the drink still made his blood run cold, but he could hardly blame her for reacting to his letter the way she had. He'd lied to her repeatedly, he'd shut her out and he hadn't given her the opportunity to try and help him. She was right, he'd been the one to ruin them in the end, not his father.

It was almost midnight when he got home. He pulled off his jacket and greeted Ziggy at the door, and spotted the photo of them in its frame, sticking out from under the bench. He should have put it up before. He'd built the cabin for her after all. He'd built everything around Jodie since he was eleven years old.

Dropping to the bench, he dusted the frame off, studying her expression in the picture, the youthful Mustang who'd been so much like Blaze. They both looked so young. He had no excuses for not hanging this picture up now, he thought…unless she really wasn't coming back.

It killed him how his own secrets from the past had messed up the future. And the sex…

that was where they'd always talked without words. Damn, he missed that. Damn, that whisky was making him feel sad. He picked up his phone where he'd left it on the couch.

Three missed calls from Emmie?

Shaking off the alcohol that Liam Grainger had forced on him, he dialled into the voicemail.

'Cole, Cole, it's me, Emmie. I'm sorry for calling you but I didn't think my mum would want to. It's Saxon, my horse, he's sick. We're at the farm with him...we don't know if he's going to make it. Can you help me, please? You're the only one I can think of who might save him.'

He crossed to the messy desk. Swiping the papers and cables aside, he located the laptop and searched for a flight.

'Dammit,' he cursed aloud at the screen. Just when he really *needed* to go to Edinburgh, there were no flights he could take before two p.m. the next day.

According to the rest of the message, Saxon had been refusing food and walking unsteadily, and now had diarrhoea at sporadic intervals, as well as excessive urination and chronic fatigue.

It sounded like some kind of poison but the vet on the premises couldn't identify it.

He only hoped *he* could, but he would have to get there fast. The overall prognosis for ionophore toxicity in horses was poor to grave... Jodie would know that as well as he did.

With Ziggy on his heels, he pulled down a bag from the closet, catching sight of his face in the bedroom mirror by the dresser.

Shaking his head at himself, he dragged a hand across his chin and witnessed himself coming full circle. It was twelve years overdue, but it was about time he got on that train to Edinburgh.

CHAPTER TWENTY

'COLE!' JODIE'S HANDS came up over her mouth
as she met him halfway across the forecourt.
'What are you doing here?'

'I hope I'm not too late.'

Cole dropped the backpack at his feet and
crossed the last foot between them. He was
wearing his plaid jacket and the jeans he always
wore in spite of having twenty pairs. The sight
of him so out of context was surreal, but suddenly it hit her... Emmie must have called him.

'She didn't tell you I was coming, huh?'

His broad shoulders seemed to hold the weight
of the world until he put his arms around her
and sighed deeply into her hair. She felt it too,
as if something lifted inside her as he held her
face in her hands. 'I missed your eyes,' he said
gruffly.

'I missed yours too. Cole, I am so, so sorry.
I totally overreacted to your letter.'

'I deserved it. I know I should have told you

everything way sooner. I was being selfish, not wanting to lose you again.'

'Well, I was being selfish too, only thinking about how I felt. You had to do what you had to do to protect me and your mum, and so did I when I married Ethan. We always wanted Emmie, Cole, and I don't regret making that decision. As for you and me…can we please start over?'

He still loved her very deeply, she could see it in his gaze. If it had been anyone else, the intensity would have made her look away, but he held her eyes like magnets, then drew her close to his chest and kissed her. For a moment as she sank into him she almost forgot why he'd come.

'Emmie,' she cried, breaking away from the kiss at the same time he released her. He slung his backpack quickly onto one shoulder over his jacket and took her hand.

'Let's go.'

In the stables Jodie watched with wet eyes as her daughter clung to Cole's middle, in tears. 'Thank you, Cole. Thank you for coming here. Can you help him?'

'Let's see, shall we?' he said, putting a steady

hand to the top of her head and throwing Jodie a look of mild surprise.

It crossed Jodie's mind that maybe Cole didn't know what an impression he had left on Emmie during the brief time she'd spent at Everleigh. Her daughter was overcome with gratitude that he'd come all the way here.

The gelding was looking very poorly indeed and secretly Jodie feared the worst. They'd all been up all night, watching him deteriorate.

'The vet just left to get breakfast with Ethan, while he's resting,' she told Cole, watching him crouch at Saxon's side. She hoped and prayed Cole would be able to reach Saxon in a different way. She'd seen him do it a hundred times with other horses, but this was different. This was Emmie's horse. If anything happened to Saxon, her little girl would be devastated.

Outside in the sunlight he accepted two coffees from a kindly woman in overalls and took one to Jodie, who was by the stables, tapping something on her phone. Saxon was now on his feet. Cole had managed to get him to stand, albeit weakly, and Emmie was over the moon.

'Ethan sends his thanks to you for you coming,' Jodie said, pushing her phone back into her pocket and dashing her hand through unkempt hair—just the way he liked it. 'You might have saved Saxon's life.'

'Tell him he's most welcome,' Cole replied. 'I'm just glad I could help.'

It transpired that poor Saxon had eaten something from the yard that had been left for the chickens. Cole had been able to tell from his stance, the way he had been pressing his belly to the ground. He'd calmed him enough to allow them to give him a second full flush and on close inspection they'd located a chicken feed container spilling into an open paddock. Luckily no other horses had tucked in.

'I don't think she'll be able to ride him any time soon. I'm sorry,' he said to Jodie in private, sipping the coffee.

'He'll need electrocardiograms and ultrasounds to monitor his heart. It's pricy stuff, and it could take time for Saxon to heal properly.'

Jodie looked determined to bring Saxon back to full health through sheer force of will. He tossed both their cups into a bin and tilted her chin up. 'Everleigh's insurance will cover it, it's tied into the inheritance. I can arrange for

Saxon to come back with me, where I can keep a proper eye on him. We can watch him round the clock until he's out of danger. You can come down whenever you're ready.'

'Are you sure?' she said, swiping at her eyes. The Scottish sun was high in the sky now, and behind her the craggy mountains looked like a movie set.

'You can both come,' he told her, hoping she'd agree. 'It's almost Easter holidays. Emmie will be close to Saxon. Meanwhile, she can ride Blaze.'

Jodie's eyes lit up. 'He's ready to ride?'

'For someone he trusts, like Emmie. Look, if you're worried about security after what happened, don't be. I had the place rigged up—'

'I'm not. But I was going to tell you before this happened, I'll press charges,' she told him, clasping the front of his jacket and pulling him closer. 'You were right, people like that need to be locked away.'

Her back was against the stable wall. She was looking at him with fierce determination and suddenly all he wanted was her, for ever. 'Do you know how much I love you? My protector?'

He pressed his smile to her forehead and she

laughed softly. 'And I love you. We'll look after each other, Cole, and Everleigh. That's what Casper wanted.'

'I think you're probably right about that.'

'And by the way, I spoke to Ethan about moving Emmie down to Dorset on a more permanent basis.'

'Oh, yes?'

'He likes the idea. But only if he can come riding sometimes.' She grinned at the look on his face. 'I think he was joking.'

'Whatever makes you happy,' he said, going in for another kiss. She put her hands up to his handsome face and realised that she'd never loved him quite as much as she did now, knowing he had finally made it to Edinburgh, not just for her but for Emmie.

'*You* make me happy, Cole Crawford.'

Eighteen months later

The lighthouse loomed behind them as Cole steered the boat, and Jodie gripped the sides in anticipation. 'Do you think they're here today?'

'They'll show us if they are,' Cole said, and she watched his profile in the loose blue shirt and blue baseball hat as he stopped the motor to reach for his camera.

They weren't here for the dolphins specifically on this sunny, warm, late September day. Toby had taken some great shots of the new Portland Bill Everleigh Suites from the land, but Cole was determined to take his own promo shots from the water.

They had more staff than ever but he still liked to do as much as possible himself when it came to Everleigh, just like Casper had always done. As if he didn't have enough on his plate, she thought in admiration.

Jodie felt the little red boat bob beneath them as Cole positioned the camera on his lap. She pulled her cardigan tighter around her, and the shimmer of her wedding ring in the sun cast a rainbow reflection on the seat.

She loved the way the different seasons brought such different opportunities for them in Dorset, from organic farming and nursing newborn lambs in spring, to inviting their guests to marshmallow singalongs round the fire pit in winter. Her veterinary duties had expanded in every way she could imagine now that Aileen had taken over at West Bow. Everleigh had never been so busy or exciting. She had a feeling it was about to get even better...once their baby arrived.

'Did Emmie tell you, she and Toby are doing their next presentation together at school?' she said to Cole, putting a hand to her swollen belly. 'They're sharing how they've been making all their own dog food from organic ingredients. It's a pretty entrepreneurial business venture, don't you think? Everleigh K9 Complete.'

'I suppose they learned from the best,' Cole said, with faux smugness. 'I know Ziggy appreciated trying out all their samples.'

Ziggy cocked his head up from the bottom of the boat at the sound of his name, and Jodie reached down to stroke his soft, warm fur. He'd been extra-protective of her since he'd sensed the baby growing inside her. 'At least they'll pay for their own college educations at this rate,' she said.

'As long as they don't stick my face on the dog-food labels, I'm OK with it.'

Cole saw her wrestling with her cardigan in the breeze and quickly reached for a blanket under the seat. 'Are you cold?'

She shook her head as he draped it across her

shoulders and laid a hand on the small bump. He was even more protective of her than Ziggy was, and every now and then she'd catch him looking at her in wonder, like he couldn't believe she was carrying life inside her—his own son. He was going to be the best father, she knew it would come naturally to him.

Five months in and she was showing through her clothes—the mums at the school were already planning her baby shower. Cole dropped a light kiss on the bump over her stretched cotton T-shirt, and she ran her fingers contentedly through his hair as he went back to looking through his camera lens.

The new Everleigh Suites looked like somewhere you wanted to be, she thought proudly. They'd had each block painted a different colour, casting a red, blue and yellow splash across the shore behind the boathouse and the paddocks.

They were already all booked out for the rest of the year—most were guests with disabled or autistic children who were engaged in animal therapy with Cole. It hadn't been Cole's plan for the space initially, but after she'd fallen pregnant, the idea had struck her, and it had stuck for both of them.

The first paying guests were due to arrive any day. They even had customised snorkels and wetsuits in the boat, and Jodie and Evie had personally arranged wine glasses and bedspreads featuring real prints of their rescue horses for the guesthouse bedrooms. The Blaze Boudoir was their best suite. He was the star horse of Everleigh after all, who only Emmie got to ride.

Jodie was lost in a dream about teaching their son to ride when a movement in the corner of her eye made them both look up. She recognised the fin instantly.

The mother of the dolphin calf they'd rescued was here.

'She's coming over,' Cole said, putting a steady hand on her knee. Jodie was mesmerised. The baby dolphin was fully grown now, at least eight feet long. She watched in awe as the pair of them swam eagerly to the boat, then leapt right in front of the bow, making her gasp. 'They haven't come that close in a long time,' she said, although she and Cole were always greeted like friends.

She leaned over the edge, feeling Cole's arm snake around her protectively. The baby dolphin was hovering at the side of the boat, its head above water, eyeing her with what she was sure was a smile. 'You can tell she knows,' Cole said, wrapping his arms around her more tightly.

'Knows what?' Jodie asked, as the creature beamed with intelligence and curiosity in the water below her.

'That you're pregnant,' Cole said. 'Did you know that dolphins can sense when women are pregnant? She's excited by the heartbeats inside you.'

Jodie turned to him in surprise as the dolphin let out a squeak and bobbed her head. Dolphins did that all the time but it looked like she was laughing. 'Is that right?' she said.

Cole took the camera up again and positioned her with the dolphin just behind her. 'Put your hands on your bump,' he said, as he started clicking the shutter in her direction.

Jodie laughed, self-conscious all of a sudden. 'What are you doing?' she said, just as the mother dolphin leapt into the air with the lighthouse behind her.

'I think we need new photos for the wall,' Cole said. 'And this moment, right now, is absolutely perfect.'

* * * * *